small white monkeys

small white monkeys
on self-expression, self-help
and shame

second edition

Sophie Collins

Book Works

CONTENTS

PREFACE TO THE SECOND EDITION
By Helen Charman ... ix
1 — CAR SICKNESS ... 1
2 — POWER OF THE CAT ... 9
    KARMA ... 16
3 — A DISEASE OF THE SPIRIT ... 17
    FAILED ATTEMPT(S) WITH FEELING WORDS ... 23
4 — OUR MOOD IS FAR MORE COMPLEX; OR, MIRRORS ... 27
    WOMEN BEGIN TO MEET EACH OTHER IN PRIVATE ... 34
    AFFIRMATION ... 41
    AFFIRMATION ... 42
5 — THE SHAPE AND FEEL OF IT ... 43
6 — AN ANGER THAT WILL POWER ME INDEFINITELY ... 53
    AFFIRMATION ... 58
7 — HAIR PIECE ... 59
    WAYS (SELF-LOVE) ... 72
    WHOSE HAIR ... 74
8 — LASTING ANGER ... 75
    THANK YOU FOR YOUR HONESTY ... 80
9 — SILENCE ... 83
    NOTES & THANKS ... 87

PREFACE TO THE SECOND EDITION
Helen Charman

Traumatic experiences have their own chronology. Trauma theory in the literary humanities intersects with the study of memory: understanding these instances is by definition retrospective, yet the process of remembering and articulating them is temporally recursive, not chronological. Conceptually, trauma is notoriously difficult to define, relating as it does to an event itself and to its repercussions: it is both external and internal at once, it both has happened and goes on happening. This thwarted linearity is powerfully related to shame, as experienced by the traumatised subject: it is difficult to dispel the belief that your inability to simply move on, travel forwards, 'get over it', is a mark of personal failure, cowardice, or inadequacy. Perhaps, your treacherous mind wonders, these negative qualities are why you allowed yourself to be harmed in the first place?

In *small white monkeys*, a significant injury is the catalyst for the psychic re-emergence of a sexual assault experienced six years prior. In fragments of poetry and chapters of prose, Sophie Collins details a thaw, a process of 'unfreezing' that is both entirely debilitating and the necessary reawakening of an 'entire part' of the brain. The monkeys themselves, a brood moving around like birds, appear at this moment of return, uncanny talismans that become symbolic embodiments of the author's shame: watching her, silently appearing wherever she goes, they cannot be avoided or ignored. The monkeys live inside a long poem, 'The Engine', the process of writing which, for Collins, becomes legible after the fact as the process of telling the story of her life.

Unfreezing through the act of writing – however circuitous a form that might take – bears many similarities to the process of psychoanalysis, a discipline that appears at several points in Collins' text. Jacqueline Rose, in an essay about Freud's loss of his favourite daughter Sophie to the Spanish flu, writes that psychoanalysis 'begins with a mind in flight, a mind that cannot take the measure of its own pain'.[1] Regardless of whether or not the desire to self-narrativize is a useful or truthful one, accessing the parts of your mind that have been frozen by a traumatic experience requires a reintegration of the painful aspects of that experience into your conscious understanding of your life, into its 'story'. You can't expel it; you have to take it into yourself, or rather, accept that it has already passed through your membranes. You might as well make it a home. This is not to say, of course, that unfreezing isn't met with considerable resistance within the text: writing about phobias – perhaps the most famous of psychic symptoms – Collins observes that in being 'cured' by exposure therapy (a stand-in, perhaps, for the exposure of self-expression), 'the owner of the phobia had surrendered something that I deemed covetable'. A phobia demands care and consideration from those around you, but the owner of the phobia, she writes, needs this care 'through no ostensible fault of her own'.

When I first wrote about *small white monkeys* in 2018, I noted that I had read the book 'in the middle of the first wave of "Me Too" allegations, a cultural moment that performed its own kind

X

of disruptive chronology'.[2] From the vantage point of 2021, the carceral logics that governed that period of time are damningly clear, and so is the liberal white feminist co-option of its radical potential. At the time, however, it was difficult to retain any kind of hold on critical thought amidst the relentless onslaught of reportage. Returning now to that piece of writing, I still recognise the woman who described herself as living at the mercy of the news cycle, waking up each morning under the threat that her day would be thrown off-course by another public story of painfully relatable experience. It is strange to begin to think of yourself as a victim so long after the moments where violation occurred. Part of the problem may be the hemming-in that occurs with victimisation: as soon as you acknowledge yourself to have suffered, you lose definition. In believing the stories of sexual violence that emerged, particularly those which identified more complex breaches of consent and more nuanced definitions of harm, you must begin to disbelieve the convenient narratives you have told yourself. *small white monkeys* is concerned with this paradox of testimony: to write about your experience is to accept the possibility of being defined by it. Still, though, the sheer fact of articulation might count more than what is being articulated.

    Both men and women can experience sexual violence, but there's a particular link between violence against women and the kind of self-expression that *small white monkeys* takes as its subject. At its heart is the question of complexity: who is allowed to be complicated? Fearing that you might be flattened out like so many others before you, against the landscape in which masculine difference is permitted and masculine wrongdoing is complex, forgivable and variable while the female binary oscillates only between madness and safety – fearing this, you have previously always hedged your bets and chosen the only option that might allow you to be serious and/or lovable. To assert your identity and strength as a woman – and the world does require assertiveness, and strength, whatever we might think of those values – you must deny your own ability to fall prey to that victimisation. It's internalised misogyny: the same kind that makes it easier not to listen to what women who testify against likeable men are actually saying and that shifts the burden of the testimony onto the teller themselves.

In Lauren Berlant's essay 'Trauma and Ineloquence', which begins with a litany of anonymous fearful testimonies – 'I am in a horrible fear' 'I fear the night' 'I am afraid to go out further than the grocery shop' 'I don't go out' – Berlant notes that trauma theorists 'turn over and over to psychoanalysis and lyric theory' in their attempts to describe the traumatic precisely because of its definitional instability: 'trauma definitionally dissolves the rules of continuity that stabilise self-knowledge over time and most because ultimately no one else can witness one's own story'.[3] The form that *small white monkeys* takes, by turns fragmentary and discursive, seems to be a practical response to trauma's failure of chronology, and also a way of sidestepping one trap of definition: if self-knowledge is destabilised then, in this text, the speaking self is too. The images, poems and mantras dividing the more conventional 'chapters' of the book allow for a kind of intersubjective voice: the 'I' that provides the lyric word games and 'Ways of Self Love' is not necessarily the same as the prosaic voice we recognise as Collins, who in turn is not a face in any of the photographs, nor the eye (or should that be I?) behind the camera. (It's important—chronologically, at least—that the book was published only a short time before Collins' first collection of poetry, *Who Is Mary Sue?*, in which the 'Mary Sue' of the title refers to the trope of a fan-fiction character being a 'thinly-veiled' version of the author).

The convergence between trauma and lyric theory that Berlant identifies is crystallised in *small white monkeys* by the central position that shame occupies in the text. Shame, Collins writes, can 'attenuate the subject's sense of self to a fatal degree, which is what makes it practically impossible, in the first instance, to discuss the traumatic event and its fallout in any conventional, comprehensible way'. It is also paradoxical: an obliteratively strong desire for self-negation that 'makes itself felt in every nerve, every brain cell and synapse that signals, paradoxically, the presence of a self'. The process of unfreezing reveals the existence of a 'renewable shame' that regenerates limitlessly as the traumatic experience is relived and relitigated by the 'council of the self'. In Denise Riley's essay 'Lyric Shame', a totemic text for Collins, Riley imagines literary writing as a way of not-speaking, or at least not speaking personally:

Why make such a bother about it, though, when anyone would naturally expect that the sense of shame would simply keep you quiet? That line of thought says it's implausible and perverse to make a noise out of the feeling of shame. However, if your shame is such that you can't manage to speak, you might be able to *write* instead. Literary writing may function, for some, exactly as a means of *not* speaking – of avoiding face to face speech all together.[4]

Here, then, a text exists as a kind of non-temporal document, one especially familiar to the lyric mode, and which serves, in part, to protect the identity of the teller. But this is an impossible paradox, something to which Riley herself frequently returns in her poetry. Take the assertion in 'Dark Looks', for instance, that 'who anyone is or I am is nothing to the work', and its contradiction a few lines later, in 'the poet with her signature' who 'stands up trembling, grateful, mortally embarrassed'.[5]

This is a conundrum, too, for the notions of solidarity and community in both trauma and in writing: crudely put, in what links self-help to self-expression. *small white monkeys* is not only a ruminative but an active text, engaged in the creation and assertion of communities of expression. If shame can function as a preventative state, *small white monkeys* confronts the terror of replacing the second person with the first, while insisting that a woman giving her testimony is never fully alone. In the face of the isolation and inarticulacy of sexual violence, this formation is a radical act: 'consider how this disaster links you in a deep and irrevocable way to many other women'. Part of this community-building project is textual, and the variety of references – Anna Mendelssohn, Ana Mendieta, Elena Ferrante, Jamaica Kincaid, Vahni Capildeo, Lisa Robertson, Artemisia Gentileschi, and more – structure and strengthen the case that Collins makes for the radical possibility present within writing itself.

       This is a kind of archival work, a redress to traditional masculine modes of canon-formation, and part of this book was written during Collins' residency, 'You Must Locate a Fantasy', at the Glasgow Women's Library. Images from the GWL archives appear in the chapter that focuses on the self-help and therapy movement that arose from the Women's Liberation Movement – particularly its consciousness raising discussion groups – in the 1970s and 80s. This feminist history is both rich and fraught – any story of the WLM is a story of intersecting and conflicting fractures along the lines of race, class, sexuality and ability – and it forms a crucial counterpoint to the literary focus of the text. (Capildeo, for example, a central poetic figure in Collins' new canon, is quoted at length in *small white monkeys* talking about their time working at the Oxford Rape Crisis Centre). This is a story of resistance that is specifically and domestically located, rooted in women's centres, refuges and rape crisis centres that often started out as squatted premises with non-hierarchical leadership structures in conflict with local councils, spaces that are now being targeted anew by trans-exclusionary public figures who wish to legislate on other people's gender. How might we tell the stories of our lives? In our books and at meal times, during bus journeys, night shifts and cigarette breaks, at the other end of a crisis phoneline.

small white monkeys ends with 'a final affirmation' that quotes Veronica Forrest-Thomson on Sylvia Plath: 'a woman who suffers can relieve her suffering by becoming the mind which creates'. The use of 'the mind' rather than 'a mind' here is crucial: this is not about individual opportunity so much as a collective reshaping of what the creative mind has hitherto been allowed to be. Within this is the potential for individualised experiences of shame to be repurposed as a kind of productivity: 'I feel my own shame hardening into an anger that will power me indefinitely'. Anger is figured here as a kind of opposite, an external rather than an internal force, and also as an alternative to the harmful repression of traumatic experiences in the service of a fiction of forgiveness, reason, or happiness. Sara Ahmed, another thinker on whom Collins frequently draws, has offered a feminist critique of happiness, arguing particularly for a black feminist consciousness, one that acknowledges what you lose or give up in following the socially conditioned pursuit of happiness. It's a critique, in Ahmed's words, that hinges on disturbing the familiar.[6]

To be productive in these terms, of course, requires vigilance against the co-option of such productivity into institutions, systems, and forms that seek to exploit its aesthetic or surface-level politics whilst reinforcing the structures that enact gendered harm. During the second long lockdown of the pandemic, a highly attenuated period of digital shame and loneliness when the closing of a laptop immediately dispersed any fragile community that had constructed itself, Ahmed gave a virtual talk at the Glasgow School of Art that introduced her new book, *Complaint!*. In it, she described the project of listening to complaint – and what is complaint if not a particular form of articulated trauma? – as the project of becoming a 'feminist ear', listening out for the ways in which making a complaint irrevocably changes the context in which you inhabit a structure, and more often than not the ways in which shame is weaponised against the complainer. The mechanisms of refusal and repression that institutions enact mimic the internal processes that trauma can instigate: a freezing, or a burial. Yet even buried complaints, Ahmed noted, have the power to haunt, to become revenant. It is crucial not to underestimate what a collective of 'lonely little ghosts' can do to a previously unassailable structure.[7] What they can thaw, what they can unfreeze, what they can finally say.

1

CAR SICKNESS

The past should go away but it never does...

And it is like a swimming pool at the foot of the stairs...

— *Poemland*, Chelsey Minnis

About three years ago I sustained an injury, a significant injury to my body, and in the wake of this my mind did something both for and against itself. I experienced what is sometimes referred to as an 'unfreezing' — that is, I reaccessed a traumatic experience, an instance of sexual assault, that had taken place six years previously, in my early twenties, the current flesh wound acting as a catalyst for this sudden thaw. Shortly, I found myself in hell. I began writing a long poem in order to manage, though I did not yet recognise the significance of this activity. 'The Engine' was a poem about another world. Inhabiting this world was a brood of small white monkeys that moved around like injured birds, like furtive healthy birds, like monkeys. There was no pretence in the poem, though it might sound impossible...

In 'friday.', Anna Mendelssohn, an important poet of zero pretence, writes,

> Poetry can be stripped. Racketeers compromise
> > advantageously
> Unracked by the objects of their disquieted attention
> Work is too much trouble to those who don't love their
> > subject
>
> And literature is lost, lost to the word work, lost to the
> > temptation
> of gradgrind rectification and its concomitant collapse...

I know I will have to work hard to explain myself, though I am racked, I am disquieted. It took me too long to recognise 'The Engine' for what it was: the story of my life until now — or quite recently. It took me longer still to recognise the monkeys for what they were, collectively: my white symbol of shame.

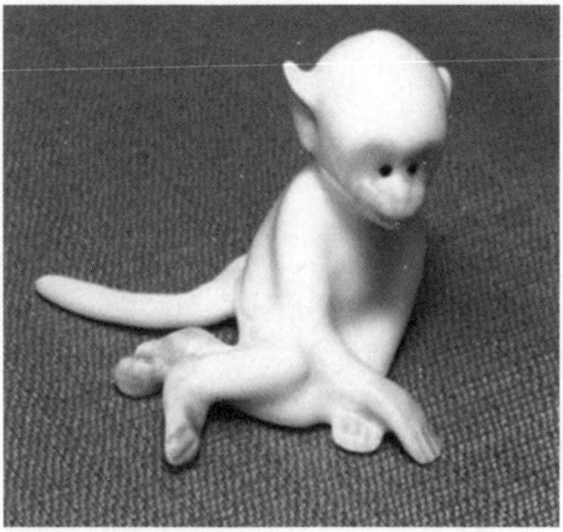

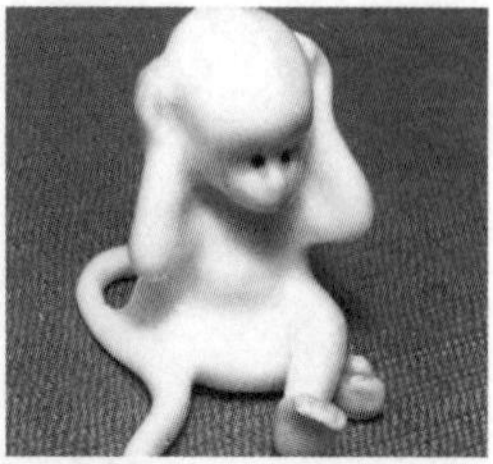

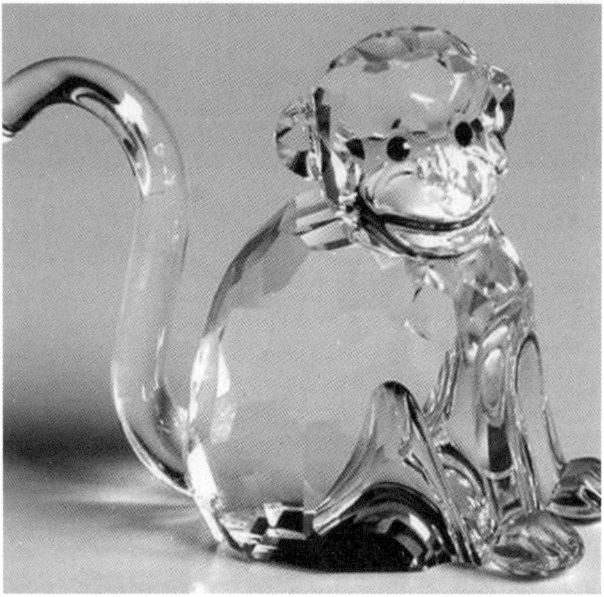

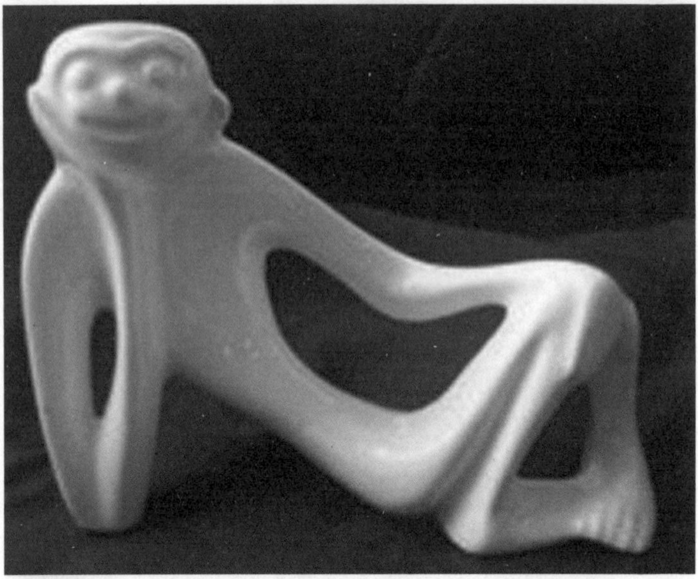

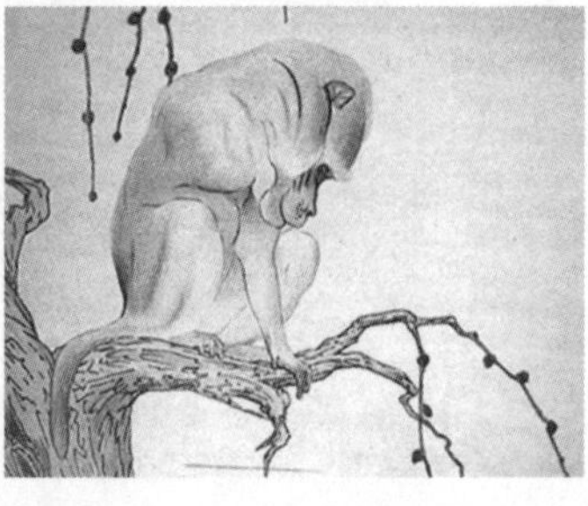

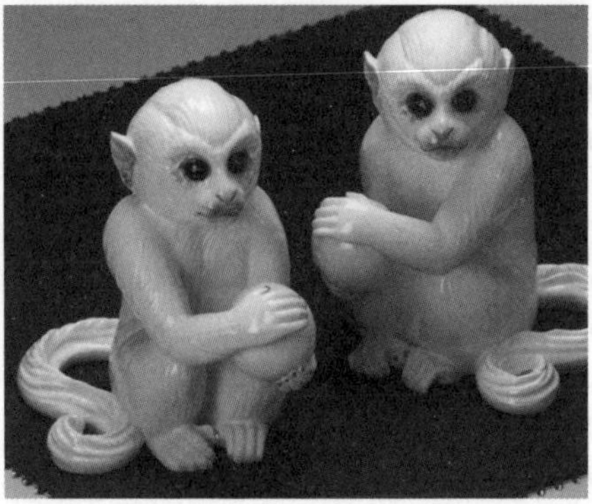

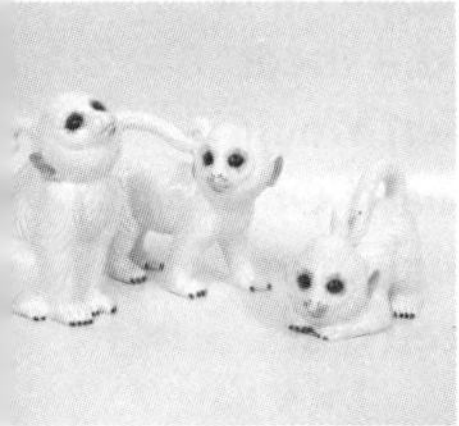

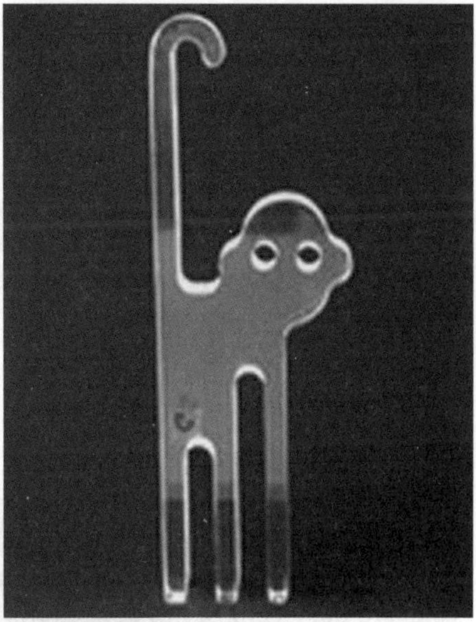

Soon after the assault I had managed to shut down an entire part of my brain while I was unconsciously at work, establishing the conditions in which it would one day be safe to reconnect with my thoughts about the event. This is not to say that I had managed to induce a wilful amnesia, only that I could bump an elbow on the corner of the memory without the least emotional or physical reaction. When thoughts of the attack and my attacker surfaced, which for a long time happened rarely, I would calmly pick up my oar and poke their unresisting bodies back into the canal's depths. I would resume life.

After the thaw, however, such thoughts became unyielding and intrusive. Repressing intrusive thoughts unleashes a series of physical effects (thirst, dizziness, inability to focus) that are in many ways worse than running through the thoughts themselves. I would worry about seeing my attacker on the street at the most implausible moments. How would I react? Would I be cordial, pretend nothing had happened (as he has)? Or pretend that something did happen, but that that something was consensual (as he has)? I tried to convince myself that nothing had happened.

When my shame and trauma were at their searing, obliterative peak, my attacker would be a peripheral figure in almost every one of my dreams, where I would move past him without addressing him.

To look at me during this time you likely wouldn't have picked up on anything. When you go through something like this you appear unchanged on the surface, but behind the skin of your face brews a nasty illness, like mercury poisoning. What can I compare the feeling of this period to?...

When I was an infant we moved abroad. Every summer we would drive through Calais to visit my maternal grandparents in the other country. I get car sick to this day, but it was at its most horrendous when I was small. We couldn't drive twenty minutes without me going pale, closing my eyes and requesting a stop, so during these very long journeys the nausea was something unbearable — I felt that it would never end. An acute and interminable nausea, then. And somewhere between the meetings and the deadlines and the social arrangements there would usually be a lay-by where I could at least stop and be sick, with some degree of privacy, before having to gather myself and move forward again.

I had to get up but I felt heavy, as though there had been a change in gravity or the make-up of my blood had somehow rearranged itself in such a way that the pull on my body now figured differently within the existing system. I kept falling asleep. In the final play of the *Oresteia*, Aeschylus' trilogy of Greek tragedies, the Erinyes — chthonic female deities of vengeance — become strangely sluggish and sleepy, and their mission to bolster Clytemnestra's desire to avenge her daughter's death falls by the wayside. On an Apulian red-figure bell-krater (an ancient black and red vase) housed in the Louvre, Clytemnestra's shade or ghost (as she manifests in the underworld) can be seen trying to rouse the somnolent Erinyes without any luck; the latter are draped over one another with their eyes closed, fully-clothed, as though they had had too much to drink at a party. Their characteristic ferocity has been deactivated, though it's not really clear how or why. Or when. My own sense, at a certain point, was one of having been incrementally plied with a cumulatively fatal poison. I wanted an antidote.

    I made it my business to read, to learn, and in this way to integrate the experience and resultant trauma into my life. But reading, as most people are aware, exacerbates motion sickness. This is because your eyes take in the sight of the book before you (as well as the interior of the vehicle in your peripheral vision) and communicate the message to your brain that you are still, while your body — sensing velocity, all the minor calibrations — states the opposite. I knew this too, of course, and so I resolved to begin gently.

2
POWER OF THE CAT

Carolee Schneemann is among the world's foremost creators of cat art. I delight in telling people about *Fuses*, a video piece in which Schneemann and her then partner have sex vertically in front of an indifferent Kitch (her then cat), or *Infinity Kisses*, a sustained project made up of photographic evidence of Schneemann's cats' daily caresses. *Infinity Kisses* began in 1981 with Cluny, the first of the artist's cats to find his human in bed in the morning (as cats are wont to do) and plant firm kisses on her mouth as though thirsting, like a lover (somewhat less usual). In a short text in *Art in America*, Schneemann speaks of her personal history with cats and of the cultural history of the species, including the well-known veneration of cats by the Ancient Egyptians and the contrasting view taken later, elsewhere:

> Cats became sacred in Egypt because they preserved all the grain by going after the mice and rats. This reverence could be very extreme. If visitors from other countries accidently killed a cat, they would be killed. Local people would readily sacrifice their lives for that of a cat. But by the time we're in medieval Europe, the cat is an obscenity; it belongs to witchcraft and unknown powers. It has to be mutilated and killed just as women who had unknown, inexplicable powers were denounced as witches, mutilated and killed. One of the ways they killed both women considered witches and cats considered to be witches' companions was to stuff the cat in the woman's vagina; the cat would claw itself and the woman.

More recently, cats have been invoked as scapegoats for cot deaths. This strange myth describes the cat, having caught the scent of milk on the baby's breath, as being heavily drawn to and inadvertently smothering the sleeping infant. In another, more vehement iteration of the same myth, the cat is said to suck the unattended supine baby's breath away with intent.

Cats love the taste of antifreeze, but the liquid's crucial ingredient, ethylene glycol, kills them painfully within hours. Cats sometimes ingest the stuff accidentally, during the winter, when it will occasionally leak from cars and spill from poorly capped bottles. But in August 2014, in Lancaster, Donald Waterworth indulged his hatred of cats by setting out dishes of tuna laced with the poison. One woman living nearby lost four cats over two weeks. Katherine Hall, 'a wealthy woman', had, in 2009, done the very same thing, killing both her next-door neighbours' cats. 'We've spent a lot of money on the garden,' said Hall in a statement. 'I wanted to stop them leaving nasty smells...'.

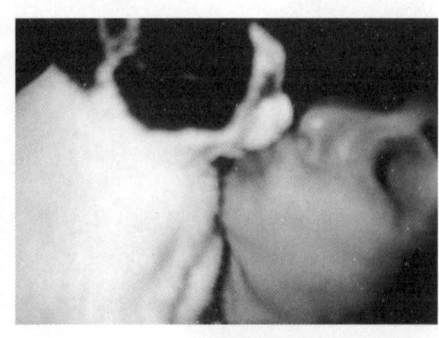

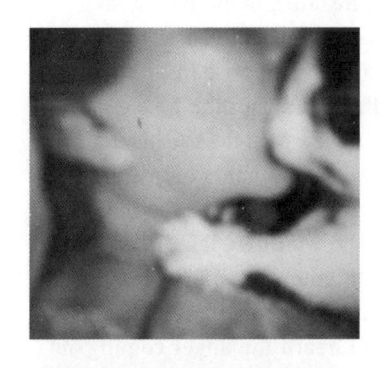

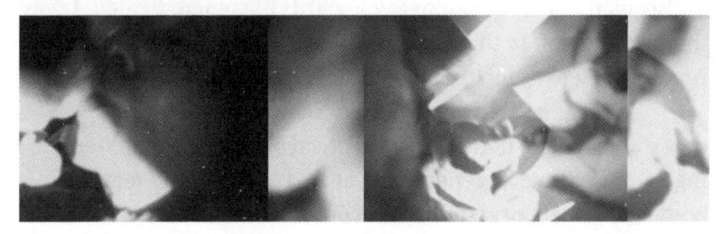

I witnessed the most remarkable instance of an individual's
revulsion of cats during my second ever visit to New York.
I had been invited to a friend of a friend's house in Brooklyn for
a drink. I'd never met the friend's friend, and the house turned
out to be a luxe four-storey town house paid for by this man's
wife's family fortune. Every weekend the man's wife and their
daughter would decamp to her parents' place (maybe in Upstate
New York or the Hamptons), and he would be left alone, in
Brooklyn, surrounded by gaudy statement art pieces in this
inordinately fancy house. I can no longer remember how the
topic of cats arose, but as soon as I heard the anger coming out
of this man I decided not to say a word; I listened, fixated. I was
the only woman in the room. 'Nasty animals, nasty animals,' he
repeated. He was looking right at me, though not with his eyes.

'In cultural history,' writes Schneemann, 'the
detestation of the domestic cat is always parallel to suppressed
rage at difference in general and at all aspects of the female
body and female orgasm in particular.'

Also Schneemann:

> It's tricky for me to emphasize the power of the cat when what surrounds its hard-to-elucidate power today is sentimental indulgence. I think such ideas are ultimately transformative, however, because the acceptance of the tenderness and thoughtfulness of the cat relates directly to the acceptance of female sexuality: its subtlety, its complexity.

My own cat looked after me until she stopped being able to eat and began lying down in her litter tray, which she was no longer really using as a litter tray because she was no longer really able to eat. I knew she would die when I saw her lie down in there: it was a shocking thing for a cat to do. She was in so much pain, she just wanted to be sucked away. We followed her wishes a few days later. The night before she died the sky was lilac.

In the years before she died, she would find me in bed in the day and we would go to sleep together in a warm knot for weeks at a time. We were time travelling. After a while she wouldn't let me sleep like this any more. She wanted me to get up in the mornings, and she made sure that I did. She wanted me up for eight.

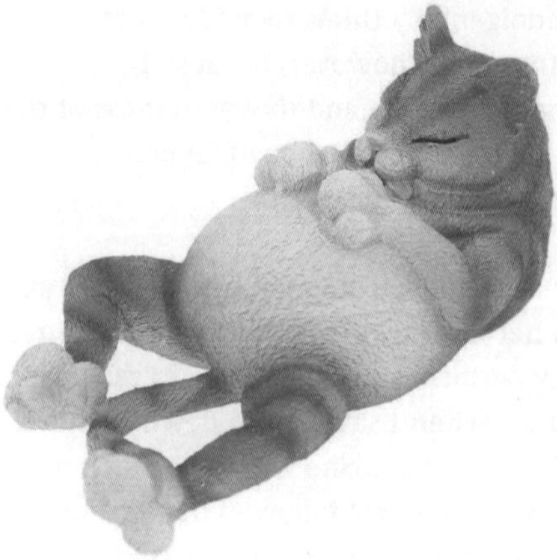

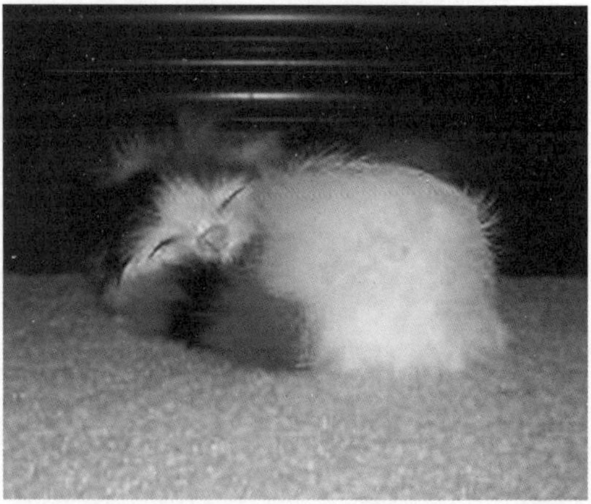

Cat thwarts sex attack on owner

S/M 19.5.94

MAX the cat thwarted a sex attacker, sinking his claws into the face of a man who attempted to assault his owner as she walked along a pathway.

The cat was trotting behind his mistress in Bracknell, Berkshire, when the attack took place. Police are looking for a man with deep scratches on his face.
— PA

KARMA

For Christmas my sister-in-law buys me a set of three perfumes, each with a different and surprising name. I cherish the perfumes; they feel powerfully symbolic. KARMA remains unopened, however: I am too fearful to apply it to myself.

3

A DISEASE OF THE SPIRIT

Shame is experienced, in a corporeal sense, as a sudden and comprehensive discomfort. Flushed with shame, we cannot excuse our own behaviour, we cannot excuse our bodies quickly enough. Because we cannot excuse our bodies quickly enough, we look away and down, bringing our hands to our faces for scant cover. Because our hands provide scant cover, we feel our skin fizz with the unwanted exposure, with newly barbed blood. Shame is everywhere and all at once, and it is most acute when we feel that we are unable to displace any element of its cause onto another.

Shame is paradoxical: a desire for self-negation — a complete abnegation of the ego — that makes itself felt in every nerve, every brain cell and synapse that signals, paradoxically, the presence of a self. In this way, shame can be fatal. Some of my most-loved writers and artists, including Simone Weil and Freda Downie, effectively starved themselves to death in the name of such self-abnegation. And there are others who came close, Virginia Woolf and Adrian Piper among them. They are the ones about whom I have the most competing thoughts, making my enjoyment of their work equivocal — this is not to their detriment.

In *The Cultural Politics of Emotion*, Sara Ahmed writes that, in shame, one attempts to retreat into the self that is nonetheless understood to be bad, meaning that, in such circumstances, the subject may feel that they quite literally have nowhere to turn: 'In shame, I feel myself to be bad, and hence to expel the badness, I have to expel myself from myself (prolonged experiences of shame, unsurprisingly, can bring subjects perilously close to suicide).' On reading these words, I thought for the first time in a long time about Jacintha Saldanha, the nurse who, in 2012, was working at King Edward VII's Hospital, Westminster, in the ward to which Kate Middleton had been admitted for intense morning sickness. Three days after appearing to fall for a prank called in via Australian public radio that gained the show's presenters access to confidential medical information pertaining to Middleton, Saldanha hung herself in her nurse's quarters, believing her actions to have put a colleague's job in jeopardy. She had no prior history of depression or ill mental health.

In the literature on shame I expected there to be competing definitions. In reality, most of the texts were tautological, both as a group and in and of themselves. Like just about everything else, the Ancient Greeks were credited with the advent of shame. As well as being deemed a 'negative affect' (along with anger, fear and anxiety), shame was frequently grouped in with other ostensibly sinful affects, such as pride or envy. Pains were often taken by the scholars and students of shame to distinguish it from its neighbour, guilt. Wisdom proffers a distinction between shame and guilt that posits the latter as a uniquely private and inwardly felt emotion, and the former as dependent on external public judgement, or anticipation thereof. In *Pride, Shame and Guilt*, Gabriele Taylor writes that 'shame requires an audience' which effectively 'constitutes an honour-group': 'often quoted are the heroes in Homer's *Iliad*. They form an honour-group: they expect certain types of behaviour of themselves and others, and judge themselves and others accordingly.'

Shame is thus broadly conceived of as deriving from a perceived discrepancy between a projected standard of how we believe we ought to be — how we *could* have been — and how we see ourselves as being in actuality. Shame might therefore be conceived of as an act of imagination — an affective state that requires the use of our imaginative capacities in the first instance in order for us to generate an idealised self-image.

I had already begun to refer to the shame I was experiencing in the aftermath of the unfreezing as 'renewable shame' — an internalised emotion, distinct from guilt, generated and perpetuated by the council of the self (an in-house honour-group, if you like). And because my shame, though bolstered by an imaginary cast, was largely internal, it eventually succeeded thoughts of the attack itself in becoming the very thing that I was attempting to conceal — from myself and others. I came across Sandra Lee Bartky's *Femininity and Domination* and her rebuke of Sartre's popular adage 'Nobody can be vulgar all alone.' 'Sartre's discussion of shame is highly abbreviated,' writes Bartky, because it evades the ways in which self can become other *within* the self, can be judged as though from the outside by the self and/or multiple, competing selves:

> Once an actual Other has revealed my object-character to me, I can become an object for myself; I can come to see myself as I might be seen by another, caught in the

shameful act. Hence, I *can* succeed in being vulgar all alone: In such a situation, the Other before whom I am ashamed is only — myself.

I felt Bartky's text looking right at me, so much so that I had to look away.

In *The Psychology of Shame*, Gershen Kaufman writes that 'intense shame is a sickness within the self, a disease of the spirit.' I kept checking my face in the evil light of the bathroom mirror for signs that might betray me.

FEELING WORDS

Abused	Delighted	Graceful
Accepted	Dependent	Gross
Afraid	Depressed	Grown Up
Aggravated	Deserted	Guarded
Aggressive	Detached	Guilty
Alone	Disappointed	
Angry	Discontented	Hated
Apathetic	Disgusted	Hurt
Anxious		Happy
Appreciated	Easy	Healthy
Appreciative	Ecstatic	Honest
Ashamed	Embarrassed	Hopeful
	Empowered	Hopeless
Balanced	Empty	Hostile
Betrayed	Enraged	Humiliated
Bitter	Enthusiastic	Helpful
Blamed	Excited	
Brave	Excluded	Important
Bored		Inadequate
	Fearful	Independent
Caring	Flexible	Insecure
Cared for	Forced	Intimidated
Carefree	Frustrated	Involved
Cautious	Furious	Included
Certain	Free	Invisible
Comfortable	Frightened	Irresponsible
Competent		Irritated
Confused	Grief	Isolated
Confident	Grieving	
Content	Glad	Jealous
Curious	Great	Joyful
	Giggly	Joyous
Daring	Gay	Justified
Deceived	Good	
Defensive	Grave	

PASA 26 Court Street suite 1209 Brooklyn, New York 11242-1102 (718) 834-9467

Kind
Kissable

Loving
Lovable
Loved
Lonely
Loyal

Mad
Mean
Miserable
Misunderstood
Moody

Needed
Nervous
Numb
Nurturing

Obsessed
O.K.
Out of Control
Overjoyed
Overwhelmed

Panicked
Peaceful
Pleased
Possessive
Powerful
Pressured
Protected
Protective
Proud

Quiet
Queezy

Rejected
Relaxed
Relieved
Rejuvinated
Respected
Responsible

Sad
Satisfied
Scared
Self-defeated
Self-doubting
Secure
Serious
Silly
Shocked
Shy
Spaced-out
Sure
Surprised
Supported
Sympathetic

Tender
Terrorified
Tingling
Ticklish
Tired
Trapped
Trustful
Trustworthy

Unhappy
Uncomfortable
Unsure

Vain
Valued
Vulnerable

Wanted
Well
Weary
Wishy Washy
Withdrawn
Worthwhile
Worried
Worthy

Yucky

Zonked

PASA: Prevention Through Education and Training

FAILED ATTEMPT(S) WITH FEELING WORDS...

...WHILE REFLECTING ON (DIS)INTEGRATION

Black
Green

Thirsty

Volcanic

...WHILE WRITING

Nobody
Needed
Nervous
Nurturing

...BEFORE HEADING TO A DINNER PARTY

Futuristic, &
Feudal

4

OUR MOOD IS FAR MORE COMPLEX; OR, MIRRORS

Not long ago I met a friend — another poet — for dinner. Among the things we discussed was a recent academic job interview in which she had been surprised to encounter, as a member of the panel (otherwise made up of literary specialists), a notable professor of witchcraft — the friend's work, creative and critical, frequently engages with the subject. She told me that one of the trickiest parts of the interview had been when this professor, who had a copy of her most recent publication in his hands, had asked her to define the term 'witch'. At that point in our conversation we must have become somehow distracted, because I found myself sending the same friend a message online a few days later, telling her that I had been wondering about the definition, frustrated by the fact that I hadn't asked her for it while we were together. She wrote back quickly: 'I define a witch as someone who uses language to make tangible changes in the material world.'

Christine de Pizan, France's (and possibly Europe's) first paid female writer, is said to have been driven to write by a similar understanding – that is, by her perception of books – things made of language – as not only aesthetic objects but powerful catalysts for material change. After her husband's death in 1387, de Pizan, who had previously written poems for her own solace and enjoyment, took up professional writing in order to look after herself and her children. The resultant texts comprised mainly moral and political tracts designed for the various dukes and monarchs who had commissioned them. Today, these manuscripts, which include *Livre de la paix* or *The Book of Peace* (composed for the Duke of Guyenne, son of Charles VI), are frequently invoked as early examples of self-help.

With the exception of de Pizan's output, the first instructive texts were made by and for men — they are known as 'mirrors for princes'. 'Mirrors' were essentially instruction manuals for patriarchs and were usually composed at the accession of a new king, when a young and inexperienced ruler was about to come to power. The best known European mirror is probably Machiavelli's *Il Principe* or *The Prince*, published in the early sixteenth century. (In modern psychology, Machiavellianism is one of the so-called 'dark triad' personality traits and is characterised by a duplicitous interpersonal style, a cynical disregard for morality and a focus, above all, on personal gain.) As prototypes for self-help guides, mirrors were thus largely designed to help men master the exertion of their powers over others.

The actual term 'self-help' originated centuries later, with Scottish author Samuel Smiles's 1859 book of that name, itself a manual on successful business and social norms in the

Victorian era. Later, as we're all aware, the genre becomes distinctly feminised (and concomitantly discredited), having significantly altered in its content. In line with the mirrors for princes tradition and Smiles's eponymous text, contemporary self-help books aimed at male buyers still impart mainly business advice and, though they are classified as self-help, do not characterise the genre as such in the public imagination. Those aimed at women, however, which concern for the most part relationships and mental health, dominate popular representations. In American films and sitcoms, anxious women in their thirties drift into the self-help sections of book shops. They browse the volumes on display there with curiosity, but are usually too ashamed to buy. Sometimes a calamity ensues as the protagonist is intercepted in the shameful act by a friend or potential love interest. Often the calamity is somehow meaningful, leading to delayed plotlines and realisations later on in the narrative arc.

The highest selling self-help books, including *Men Are from Mars, Women Are from Venus*, *You Can Heal Your Life* and *The Secret*, all offer models for living and/or allude to the existence of an obscurely defined cure-all. Both formulas present readers with the possibility of a future moment of self-actualisation that the books themselves do not possess the means to ensure.

Sara Ahmed has written that happiness is merely a 'promise' tendered 'for having the right associations'. In self-help texts, men are encouraged to uncover money and women are too, though the latter are offered additional bromides in a spectrum of hues, 'secrets' that encourage the reader to defer any genuine act of self-reflection, propelling her, rather, towards capitalist participation (via 'positive thinking') and the assembling of a nuclear family (through the instilment of gender essentialist values). *The answers are within you*, intone the books, while effectively indicating the opposite.

Excluded from dominant perceptions of the self-help

genre are alternative strands of feminist and queer publications that began to surface in volume in the 1970s and '80s. These texts offered practical advice on matters of mental and physical health, and health care and legal systems, as well as perspectives and psychological insights that might establish in their readers a long-term sense of bodily and mental autonomy. Sheila Ernst and Lucy Goodison's *In Our Own Hands*, published in 1981, was written specifically in order to provide women with the tools to establish their own therapy groups, espousing an approach that was lambasted in the mainstream media of the time as unnecessary and self-indulgent. From the book's introduction:

> One of the keystones of the new and stronger women's liberation movement which re-emerged in the radical upsurge of the late sixties was the small, informal consciousness-raising group. Here women met to talk and learned that what had previously seemed an individual problem was, in fact, a common problem shared by many. We learned that these experiences were the product not of individual failure but of the contradictory demands society makes on all women....Women involved in the movement were generally happier, more confidently active, braver and more angry.

In adopting this format alongside other therapeutic approaches, including those 'developed by men' ('as feminists, we approach them critically'), Ernst and Goodison write that they and other women have 'become better able to deal with contradictory desires: between wanting to be active and independent and wanting to be cared for; wanting to be intimate with others but not wanting to be swallowed up.' Therapy, they assert, can help us to understand 'the resources we have within ourselves', enabling us to 'more actively give and receive love'.

'Attention is the rarest and purest form of generosity,' writes Simone Weil in *Gravity and Grace*. I once typed out the following words to a friend: 'I take your book recommendations seriously because I love you.'

There is an addictive intimacy to all-women environments, a separateness that feels important, even in text. This is something I probably experienced for the first time while reading Judy Blume's young adult fiction *Are You There God? It's Me, Margaret*. I didn't hear the book — my first introduction to both menstruation and religious agnosticism — spoken about until some way into my twenties, when I began to consciously understand it as something surreptitiously passed from woman to girl, or else left on an unassuming shelf in a holiday rental otherwise occupied by furry-edged board games — a kind of dead letter box for such artefacts. Today, I get this same buzz from friends and events and writing and visual art, of course, but also from editorial and translation work. At a literary translation conference in Seattle, Kim Hyesoon was asked what she thought of Don Mee Choi's English-language translations of her Korean poems. 'It is like meeting someone like myself,' she answered. From her perspective as a translator, Choi describes the process of translating as something equally 'born from twoness'.

There is also — still — a shock and a delight in seeing female experiences named, and both the establishment of women's networks and the naming of these experiences contribute to the consciousness-raising that can combat the silence and the dampening of the self that pervade trauma. Indeed, it is in looking at other women that I feel I am able to see myself most clearly, a sentiment that is manifest in Christine de Pizan's most celebrated text, *The Book of the City of Ladies*. At the opening of the book, de Pizan relates a vision in which she is visited by the notional figure of Lady Reason. Having been launched into an acute state of self-digust by Matheolus' *Lamentations*, a thirteenth century text in which women are presented as uniquely jealous and malicious, Lady Reason asks de Pizan to consider whether Matheolus' claims mirror her own experiences of women. After attesting to the ostensible fallaciousness of Matheolus' account, de Pizan embarks on a revision of the narratives of hundreds of prominent female figures from throughout history, including Isis, Mary Magdalene and Helen of Troy.

A potentially trite observation: when it comes to the integrating of trauma into your life — because that is what can and should be hoped for — all help is self-help. Others (friends, partners, animals) can significantly aid in the process, but the difficult reorganisation required by the psyche is all applied 'self-work' that involves a sometimes excruciating self-directed attention. This must surely be one of the hardest and most confrontational acts of love.

Much of my time in therapy following the unfreezing was leading me towards a realisation that, while I had consciously adopted the feminist principles that allowed me to absolve other women of guilt in instances like that in which I now found myself, I continued to disallow myself the internal release that would derive from yielding to that same absolution. And even this realisation did not constitute its own endpoint, for such things are rooted in years of thought and experience, reaching back even to a time when the self and the world were experienced without words. The realisations will be ongoing: they will never stop, and I will never stop seeking them, though I understand that they will often be the cause of pain and of considerable anger. I understand this, at least in part, because I have read it. From *In Our Own Hands*:

As we were changing we found we were frequently feeling angry. This surprised us and embarrassed us. We had grown up feeling that we needed to love everyone and be loved by everyone. If we got angry with someone or they with us, we felt in some sense that we were failures. There were many ways we had learned to cover up our anger. Many have accused us of being shrill. Our mood is far more complex. Our critics hear only the anger, and anger separated from real issues is a distortion. The anger that is in us is a starting point for creative change and growth.

WOMEN BEGIN TO MEET EACH OTHER IN PRIVATE

they talk about the powerful myths
Susanna
Susanna
Susanna
Susanna
Susanna
the excitement and the closeness
two women
wolf and chick
massive contradictions between the absolute need for self-determination
and the guilt for wanting it

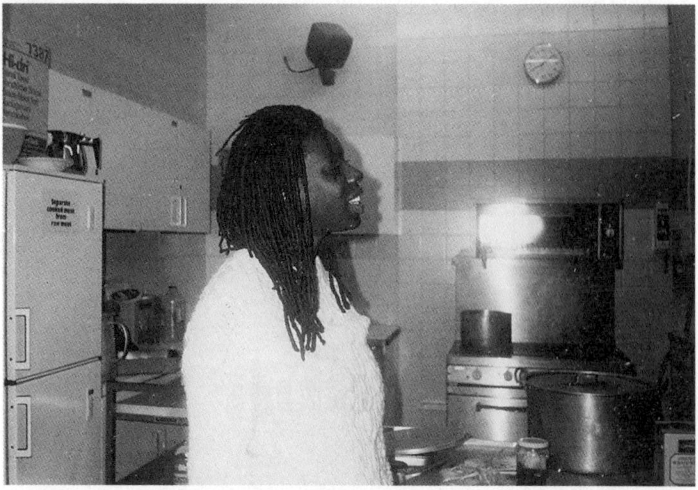

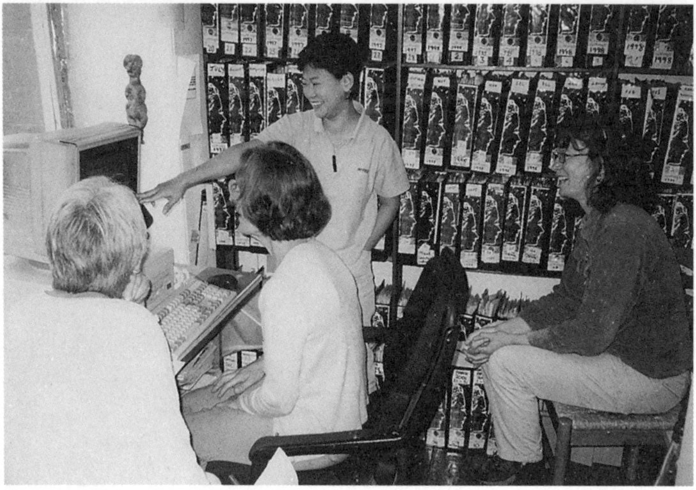

we object!
Defend
lesbian & gay
rights
GLASGOW LESBIAN AVENGERS
WE
RECRUIT

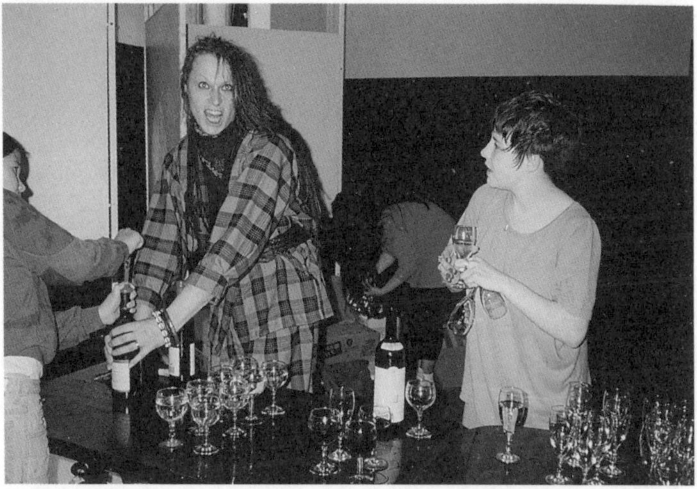

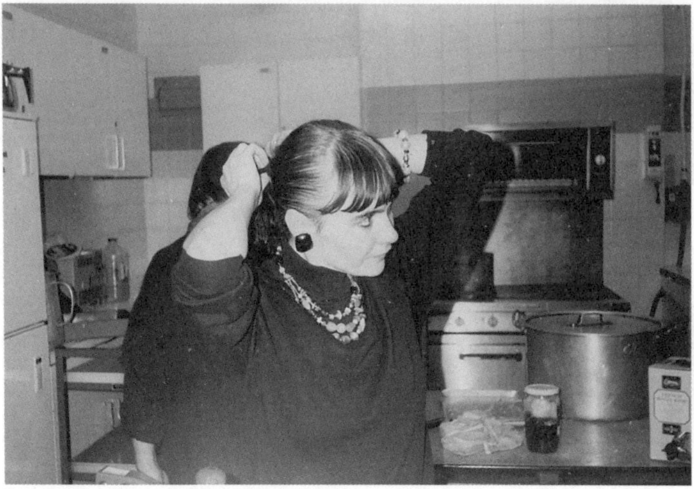

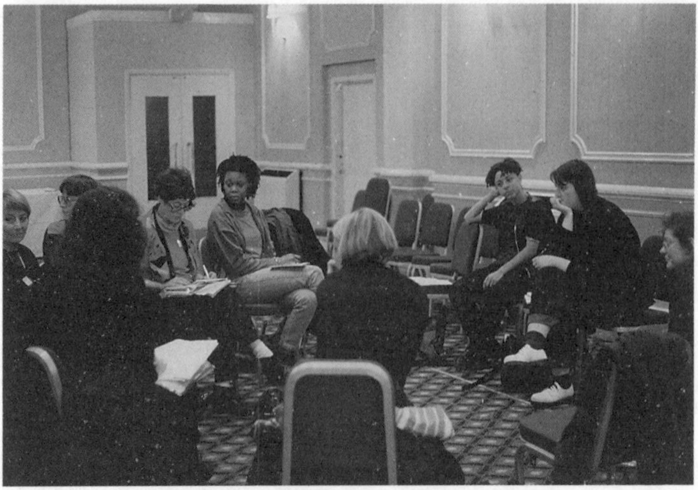

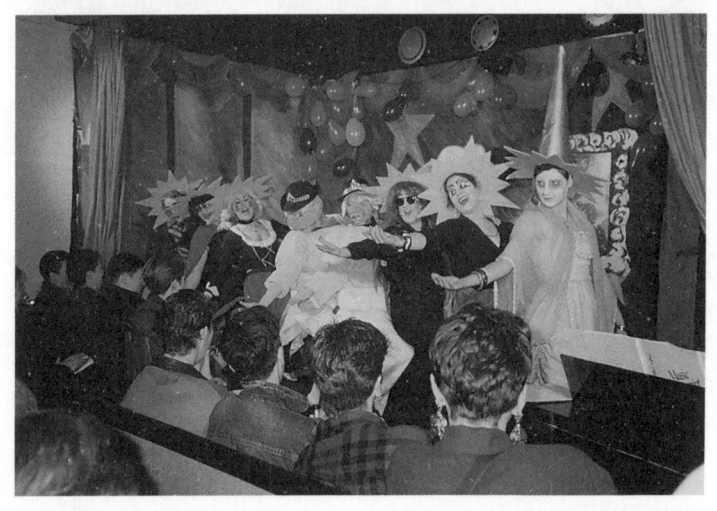

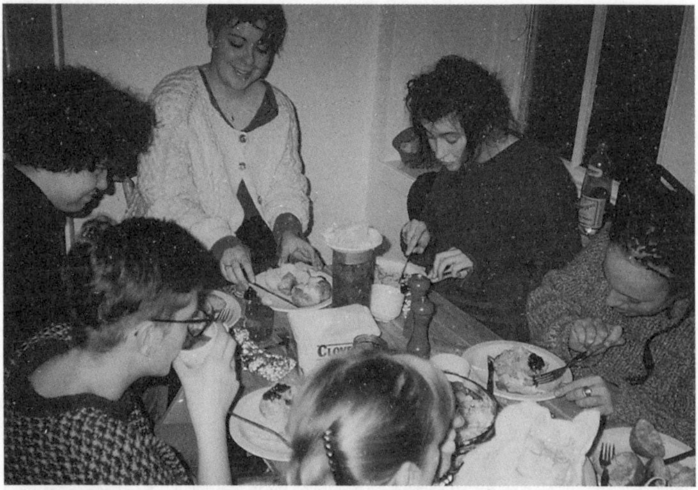

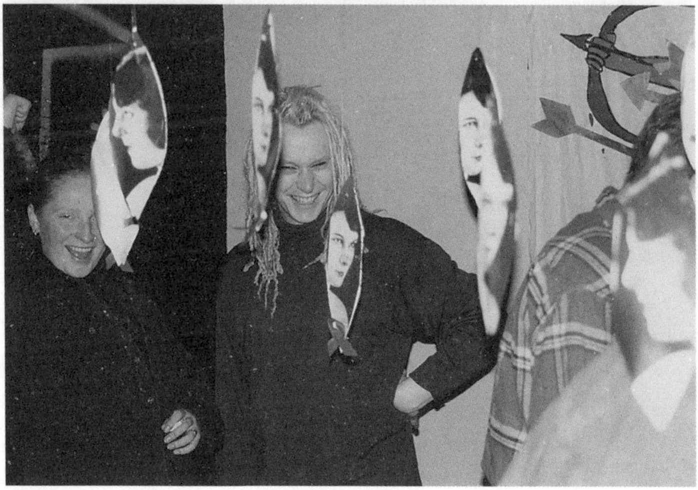

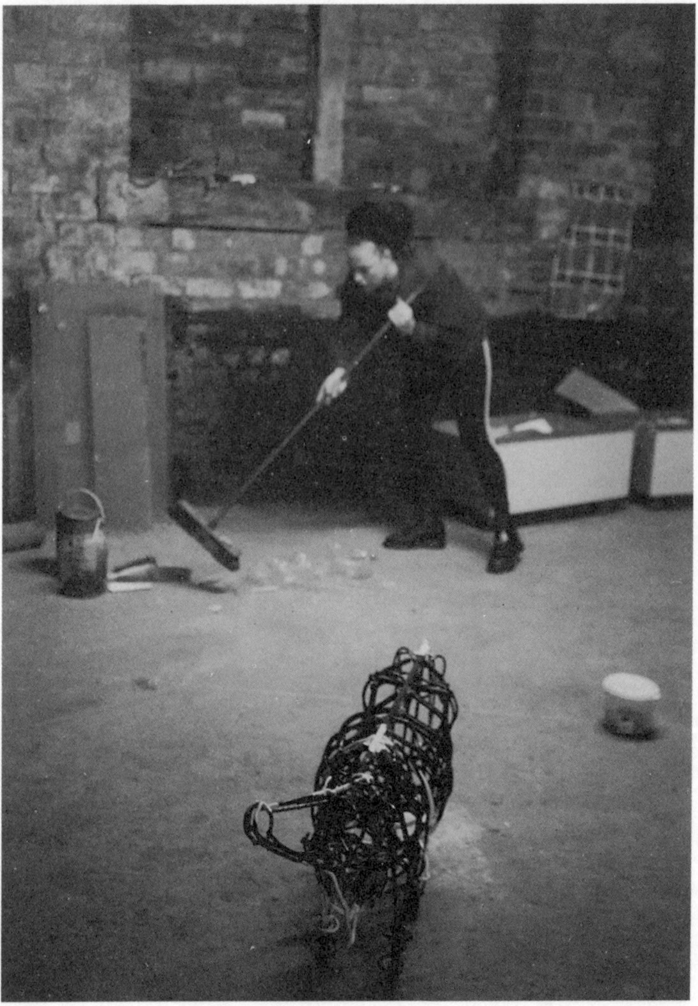

AFFIRMATION

I am not wrong: Wrong is not my name.

AFFIRMATION

I am smaller, uglier, more powerful than before.

5

THE SHAPE AND FEEL OF IT

If legal punishment has not been sought or secured, you might harbour a fantasy in which your attacker consciously faces their crimes, is crushed publicly in the most mortifying, excoriating way, obliterating everything (relationships, career) that brings them the enjoyment, satisfaction and comfort they do not deserve. But living out this fantasy carries with it the possibility of having to face a public yourself (less than desirable). Because if shame is still present (can it ever be fully eradicated?), exposing its source feels akin to exposing your inescapable flaw and so, it might seem, revealing the extent of the discrepancy between our projected and 'real' selves — a mortifying thought for someone already mired in self-generated shame. Internally, then, the flaw constitutes a metaphorical mark of shame, though such things have, throughout history, been realised in actual and horrendous ways. There is the medieval 'mask of shame', which is less like a mask and more like a helmet — a copper-coloured rendering of the shell of a pig's head, complete with ears and a long hard snout (the whole thing fastens around the neck). The white 'dunce cap' worn by Victorian schoolchildren is another, likely more familiar example. Punitive depilation of men, especially the burning off of pubic hair, was used as a mark of shame in some ancient Mediterranean cultures. Women who committed adultery have been forced to wear specific icons or marks, or have had their heads shaved to induce shame through the invitation tendered to public abuse.

Apart from any temporary or lasting damage to the ego, it's conceivable that revealing one's perceived flaw might also constitute a realistic threat to one's life (relationships) and livelihood (via public image) that is not solely the product of paranoid thinking. I imagine myself looking into the artist Adrian Piper's *Everything #4*, an oval, wood-framed mirror on which the words EVERYTHING WILL BE TAKEN AWAY are uniformly printed...[†]

In another piece, a performance work titled *Catalysis IV*, Piper went about her way in Manhattan with a towelling rag stuffed in her mouth, puffing out her small cheeks, a white plume of it left hanging out down her chin like suspended vomit. The photo documentation shows those around her continuing their conversations or looking fixedly away — responses that could just as easily be a gesture of politeness — solidarity, even (why make a stranger uncomfortable by asking potentially unnecessary and invasive questions?) — or a solipsistic lack of care.

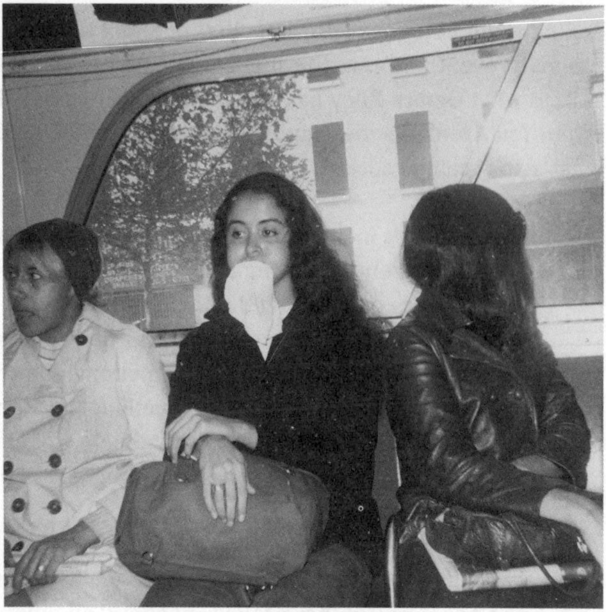

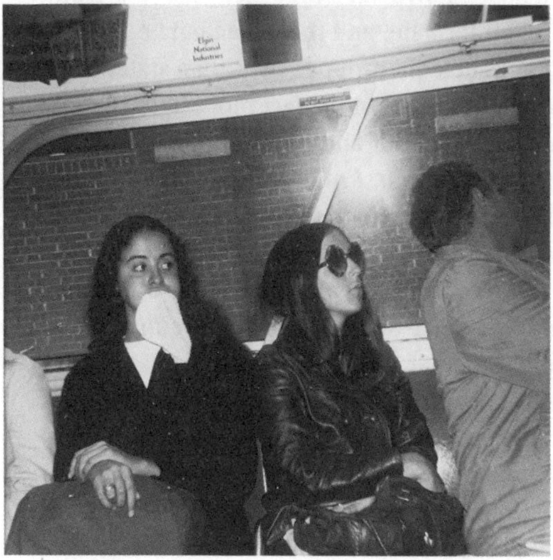
Elgin
National
Industries

Telling about being sexually assaulted — and, I suspect, any traumatic event — forces the speaker to experience something akin to what Denise Riley has articulated in her essay '"Lying" When You Aren't' as 'the impossibility of truthfully inhabiting what's an accepted social lie':

> Here I don't mean that old and time-honoured business of deliberately conveying a lie through the flawless contrivance of speaking the literal truth. Nor do I mean the truthful alibi, where the alibi is a self-conscious assertion which masks the real emotional dimension; its literal truth is belied by its situational untruth. What I have in mind, rather, is that feeling of emitting an aura of lying, and the corresponding fear of not being believed.

As an example, Riley offers a familiar scenario in which she finds herself reneging on her promise to attend an imminent social gathering due to an oncoming illness. On making the call to her prospective hosts, however, she realises that her truth will no doubt be taken for a lie, and that an actual lie — say, that a friend has unexpectedly dropped by, is in a state, cannot and should not be left alone — will in fact more likely be taken for the truth. Thus an 'accepted' and 'social' lie, given that the phrase *I'm sorry I can't make it, I'm coming down with something* is most often understood to *be* a lie, as well as constituting some kind of social currency, handed back and forth as suits the needs of those deploying it. 'The truer the excuse she uttered, the more acute her own bad conscience,' Riley states, is a paradox that, true to her chosen example, frequently seems to arise from 'the most everyday of excuses'. The social status of the sexual assault claim, however, might constitute one of the more grave instances in which this same principle holds just as well. This is due to the fact that, just as the 'truthful social excuse is suffered all the more acutely because it is riddled with its speaker's *unconscious* guilt' (which derives, at least in part, from 'the dominating presence of a linguistic formula'), the rape claim is often infused with an *unconscious* guilt or shame, which can exist entirely separately from, and in addition to, any emotions experienced at surface-level.

Elsewhere, Riley discusses the inability of speaking the 'I' at all if you happen to possess a general sense of confusion or fraudulence when it comes to the assertion of a firm identity. This sense of an inner divide, of possessing a non-essential self, is particularly pertinent in the context of sexual assault, given that such an attack constitutes not only a breach of your personal physical boundaries but on the self's psychic borders. Rather than being the result of an intellectual resolution that could have been arrived at decisively and empoweringly, this split or rupture is, in the wake of assault, experienced as something violent, beyond the subject's control.

Shame can thus attenuate the subject's sense of self to a fatal degree, which is what makes it practically impossible, in the first instance, to discuss the traumatic event and its fallout in any conventional, comprehensible way: if you can no longer perceive yourself as a self, how can you put 'I' in front of a verb, how can you join several of these sentences together, when asked? How can you formulate a coherent testimony, one that 'reads well' in legal and personal contexts, that causes others to 'read' you 'well', i.e., as a legitimate, perhaps even *ideal* 'victim'? In a recent podcast interview, Vahni Capildeo invoked the myth of Kassandra as a prelude to this very discussion. Kassandra is said to have possessed prophetic powers, which had been gifted her by the god Apollo as part of his efforts to seduce her. Later, when she spurned his advances, Apollo spat straight into Kassandra's mouth, activating a curse that meant that, from that moment on, nobody would believe a word she said. Capildeo:

I started thinking of who else doesn't get listened to, and then I also started thinking of my own work with Oxford Rape Crisis years ago, and I realised that it can be that if you have a visionary narrative, or if you have a narrative which seems in any way fragmented, people actually don't know how to hear that. It's another way of returning to that 'looking without seeing', or listening without hearing — that if there isn't actually the willingness to enter a space of hearing of prophetic narrative, then perhaps it just sounds violent or distorted or gabbling, which is like what happens if someone tries to report a rape, and they can't tell you, 'Well at 6 o'clock this happened, then at 8 o'clock this happened, and then at 8 o'clock the next day I thought this and I felt that, so at 9 o'clock I rang you.' If they don't present a sort of linear narrative they often get punished, because the amount of violence and fragmentation that they convey is something that doesn't fit people's ideas of a witness...

Presently, the individual publicly expressing shame might not have to contend with being disbelieved as such, but with accusations — particularly when it comes to writing — of touting trauma in exchange for (cultural) capital, or simply in order to afford their image a sense of depth. In the TV series *Westworld*, a theme park is populated by highly advanced animatronic robots referred to as the park's 'hosts'; the latter are deemed to be more believable to their human 'guests' if they are programmed to call on and communicate experiences of trauma.

In a different essay, 'Lyric Shame', Riley begins with a few lines from a poem by W. S. Graham titled 'What Is the Language Using Us For?': 'Certain experiences seem to not / Want to go into language maybe / Because of shame or the reader's shame.' This seems to be both a comment on the theoretical stance that understands all language as metaphor (perhaps the only thing that language can accurately portray is the *attempt* at expression) as well as the idea that certain affects are — due to their nature — perhaps simply more 'translatable', more suitable to language than others. Of all the emotions, shame seems to be particularly unsuited to self-expression given that both the action of writing and the affective experience of shame involve radical processes of self-abnegation. Another well-known principle: when two lines set at matching angles move away from us and towards each other, into the distance, what we get is a vanishing point.

Because it is resistant to being put into language, shame becomes restless and mutable in description. In Elizabeth Strout's story collection *Anything Is Possible*, shame is depicted both as a sausage skin and as a needle. It is internal and external — something that encases the subject in a pearly film, rendering her movements slow and jagged, as well as a sharp object, one that can pierce the subject's body and get lodged there, in her chest, where it will sit next to her heart like a hairball. Shame can also exist independently of our bodies — it needn't physically touch us. Selima Hill has shame as a white balloon, and Nuar Alsadir as a dog. Both dog and balloon require us to animate them, to keep them alive, to give them a degree of credence: we must feed and walk and touch them, we must blow them up with some effort in order to change their object status from passive to active.

A lot of people are scared of needles and dogs, and it seems likely that shame in writing might adhere to the shape of a widely feared object. As a self-diagnosed hypochondriac, I had always hoped that I might develop a bona fide phobia. I remember watching TV documentaries when I was young in which subjects underwent exposure therapy in the hope of eradicating their phobias, which typically concern a particular situation (enclosed/exposed spaces), object (a mushroom, for example, or a needle), or animal (rat, snake, cat). The full-blown phobia can be differentiated from everyday fear by the disproportion between the actual danger presented by the situation/object/animal and the measures taken by the individual with the phobia in order to avoid it. Women are twice as likely as men to develop a phobia. The logic of exposure therapy is that as the individual is repeatedly exposed to their phobia with nothing bad coming of it, they will begin to see the exaggeration of the degree to which they perceive the situation/object/animal to be dangerous. At the point in the documentary at which it was revealed that the individual was no longer phobic (she is often pictured handling a kitten or tarantula), I remember experiencing the opposite of a climax that was not exactly an anti-climax (given the absence of a conventional narrative build), but pure disappointment. The owner of the phobia had surrendered something that I deemed covetable. Which was what, exactly? A phobia not only made someone unusual, but someone who had to be catered for, looked after and considered, through no ostensible fault of her own.

But what of the phobia's source? In a recent text titled 'Unknowing', poet and psychoanalyst Nuar Alsadir describes walking into her kitchen one morning to find the remnants of a rodent's nocturnal activities — a broken-into food packet, a tiny pile of tiny shit pellets. A full-blown phobia ensued, though Alsadir had no previously acknowledged fear of rats or mice. In fact, she said, they tend to represent knowledge in her cultivated, personal mythology, 'but the knowledge that is unknown, the unknown knowns, *the unspoken, which slips like a mouse between dreams*'. After a session with her own analyst, however (psychoanalysts are required to attend their own course of analysis for a minimum of three years as part of their professional training), it became clear that the phobia was, at its core, misdirected aggression deriving from the perception that there were certain people in her life who were – albeit metaphorically – 'shitting' all over it:

> But aggression is an unacceptable emotion, according to my superego. What would it say about me if I were aggressive? By splitting off my aggression and projecting it into rodents, I was able to create phobic objects that contained all of the unacceptable feelings that had once been inside of me.
>
> ...
>
> Horses, rodents, phobic objects are not the source of fear, but the vehicle through which aggression, sexual desire and other id impulses flagged by the superego can be avoided.

To my mind, the worst fears and phobias, the worst images, like Alsadir's rodents, all transmit a sense of the object's — and so too the associated id affect's — uncontainability. In Jean Rhys's autobiography *Smile Please*, I remember being struck by Rhys's retention of the following dream-like image from her childhood in Roseau, Dominica, in which a centipede's uncontainability — its own ability to split — is shown to be part and parcel of its indestructability:

> Meta [my nurse] told me that if a centipede was killed all the different bits would be alive and run into corners to become bigger, stronger centipedes. It must be crushed. She said 'mashed up'. To this day I'm not quite sure if I really saw two halves of a centipede walking away from each other, still alive.

And so here the white monkeys — multiple, though homogenous (even monochrome — though mainly white, perhaps due to the possibility of being taken for a lie), and always present, at a distance. Agile, sentient, uncanny, diffuse — uncontrollable; pale storehouses for the superego's banished shame.

Shortly after she had heard me read 'The Engine' aloud at a literary event, a friend of mine reported having seen two white monkeys scrabbling about on a factory roof in industrial Glasgow. Though of course it was a hallucination, she quickly added — as she got closer to the building, it became obvious that the white monkeys were in fact two large white cats. But what was strange, she said, was that both animals had somehow been left with stumps for tails. Another friend recently sent me, via text, an image of an African tapestry in which a monkey is trying to tear a cloth covering from a woman's head, prizing it away with one monkey hand, its two monkey feet planted on her hunched shoulders for leverage. A week or so prior to my receiving the text, a man had walked past me in the street adjacent to my building. 'There's a monkey on my back,' he had muttered into his chest, over and over again.

6

AN ANGER THAT WILL POWER ME INDEFINITELY

The reality for many female writers and artists who have been subject to men's violence is an encoding — of shame and a desire for revenge, and of the circumstances that produced that shame and hatred — into their work. Artemisia Gentileschi, a painter working in seventeenth century Rome, was raped by her tutor Agostino Tassi (another man, Cosimo Quorli, was also implicated). After the assault, Gentileschi became sexually involved with Tassi, believing that his eventual marrying of her would restore her honour and secure her a future that would otherwise be difficult, given that Tassi had taken her virginity in the initial attack. A little while later, however, Tassi reneged on his promise to marry Gentileschi, and Gentileschi's father, who had presided over both her mentorship by Tassi and the marriage arrangements, took Tassi to court. At the end of the seven-month trial, which centred on Gentileschi's loss of virginity (she and her father would never have been able to bring the case to court were it not for this detail), Tassi was sentenced to one year in prison, which he never served. During the trial, Gentileschi was subjected to a gynaecological examination and torture (using thumbscrews) to verify her testimony.

Gentileschi's depictions of women killing men stand out because now, as then, representations of women harming or even simply intimidating men are rare, while images of the inverse are — were — so prevalent as to go unnoticed in this regard. But I believe it is depreciating Gentileschi's oeuvre to undermine what is, without doubt, its intensified bloodlust, to put the perception of the latter down purely to matters of contrast. In what is probably Gentileschi's most widely distributed painting, *Judith Slaying Holofernes*, Judith and her maid are in the thick of beheading a supine Holofernes with a sword. The women are both relatively young (in other renderings the maid is usually portrayed as an old crone) and both are red and wrinkled with focus and the application of force. Blood emits from Holofernes' neck in thick reams, like steel wires.

In Gentileschi's first ever painting, *Susanna and the Elders*, which was made a year or two before the rape trial, Susanna's repulsion and terror in the face of the elders' sexual attentions is palpable in her crumpled facial expression and general physical demeanour; her neck is held at a painful angle in her attempt to evade physical contact with the two older men, who visibly egg each other on — they look drunk. There are a number of strikingly dissimilar renderings of the same biblical scene by other Baroque artists, each of which shows Susanna either making direct eye contact with the elders or gazing aesthetically into the middle distance, somewhere above the viewer's head. In Peter Lely's depiction Susanna faces her accosters with a doe-eyed innocence, while in Sisto Badalocchio's painting Susanna is positively serene, her mouth forming a small 'o' (she could be singing). In her own later version, made just over a decade after the first, Gentileschi's second Susanna remains turned from the elders' gaze, but her expression is now one of a subdued exasperation. Her body is more or less covered with the sheet that, in the earlier painting, lies ineffectual across her left thigh.

In my favourite of Gentileschi's paintings, *Judith and her Maidservant*, made around the time of Tassi's trial, Judith stands opposite her maid, who wears a yellow dress. The sword Judith has recently used to slay Holofernes has been cleaned and is slung over her shoulder in a casual gesture, though her grip of its handle remains tight. The maid, still young, carries a wicker basket, and in the wicker basket is Holofernes' head, its skin a washed-out chartreuse. The whole effect is one of a conversation between mistress and maid interrupted — both women look to the right of the painting as though responding to a call or harking the opening of a nearby door. Despite the hierarchy of roles laid out in the painting's title, the women are casual with one another. Judith has a protective hand on her maid's shoulder, her outstretched arm doubling up as a shield to block Holofernes' decapitated head from the interloper's view.

Reading more about the details of Tassi's trial, I come across something about the involvement of another woman, Tuzia. At the time of Gentileschi's attack, it seemed that Tuzia — a young woman, though older than Gentileschi at the time — was renting an apartment above Gentileschi's home, where the assault took place. On the day of the attack, Artemisia recorded having cried out for Tuzia's help, which was something Tuzia likely heard but opted to ignore. On reading this, the sense of solidarity in Gentileschi's painting feels all the more hopeful — and painful, too, for that hope.

At times I am desperate to know more about Gentileschi's internal life and affective experiences in the wake of her attack. Her work is so lucid and aggressive as to appear to preclude self-doubt as a response; I hold her up as a beacon. 'The most typical affects observed to follow shame,' writes Kaufman, 'are *fear, distress* (the crying response, more commonly called sadness) and *rage* (an intensification of anger affect).' In 'Lyric Shame' Riley writes of her own distress: 'my own aim is to finally convert "shame" into a bearable sadness. When the pressure of shame itself can become a productive force, the lyric poem might sometimes just be one way of enacting and demonstrating this conversion...'. Ultimately, Riley believes in shame as a sadness that can be sung. I feel my own shame hardening into an anger that will power me indefinitely. Ana Mendieta, another artist, believed that all art comes out of sublimated rage — 'rage and displacement'. I am angry because I have been ashamed for that of which I ought not to have been made to feel ashamed, and, as I now know, anger is a battery. From an interview with poet Lisa Robertson:

> I think that anger indeed can become productive. Especially if one gives oneself the space for reflection too. And certainly anger can aerate the debilitating

sadness that is another response to the rampant institutional misogyny that structures much public and commercial discourse.... Sometimes to wake up and eat and work is an action that can require all affective reserves, including anger. It is a fact that women are often punished for expressing anger, subtly or otherwise. I know that in my life I have sought out women's anger.

AFFIRMATION

I have begun to recognise a source of power within myself.

7

HAIR PIECE

I can talk about blood and hair much more easily that I can talk about abstract things like anger or fear...
— Selima Hill, interviewed by Lucy Winrow

Saved, rescued, fished-up, half-drowned, out of the deep, dark river, dry clothes, hair shampooed and set. Nobody would know I had ever been in it. Except, of course, that there always remains something. Yes, there always remains something....
— *Good Morning, Midnight*, Jean Rhys

I went to New York a third time. Halfway through the trip the temperature in the city dropped from plus fifteen to minus ten degrees Celsius and stayed there. My hands and ankles became chapped and dry, and another effect was that my uniform — my long blue skirt and tights — became covered in static. Everything I touched snapped, my clothes crackled as I walked and stray hairs moved onto me from every floor and seat and stayed there. I pulled small knots of stray hairs too dark and variegated to all be my own from my skirt hem upwards of five times a day. When I took my clothes off in the evening (*crackle*, *pop*) there were hair knots attached to the thighs of my tights, to my calves and even inside my underwear — strangers' hair inside my underwear, between my cheeks. There was nothing I could do about it, and I felt shabby — a feeling that lasted for weeks afterwards.

My designs for this penultimate passage began with the following outline: 'a comparative analysis of representations of hair in Selima Hill's *Bunny* and Jean Rhys's *Good Morning, Midnight*'. Accordingly, I began to write something about hair and renewal. In Rhys's novel there is a pervasive sense of the new hairdo as salvation. New hair is money, public approval, autonomy — a direct counter to wretchedness. The narrator Sasha — who finds herself alone, in Paris, in dire circumstances, in the wake of a broken marriage, a dead baby and more — chatters to herself endlessly about when, about what colour... She wants to become a blonde cendré (an ash blond), which is of course the most difficult to achieve artificially... In *Bunny*, Hill's book-length sequence of poems that detail the adolescent speaker's abuse at the hands of a sickly, spectral 'lodger', hair is not the symptom but the source of shame: the speaker wears a damp balaclava to bed at night ('like some old ship') to flatten out her hair, her curly hair which the lodger has told her is beautiful and which she therefore understands as inviting his unwanted attentions...

I soon became aware, however, that, in attempting to shape my thoughts about these books into an 'intelligible', collective 'statement about the non-verbal world', I was enacting what literary critic Veronica Forrest-Thomson terms 'bad Naturalisation'. In *Poetic Artifice*, her ground-breaking study of poetry, Forrest-Thomson argues for practices of close-reading that operate *against* the treatment of poems as texts that are simply 'engaged in the language-game of giving information' — intricate riddles to be wrested of their essential, instrumental message. *Bunny* and *Good Morning, Midnight* are among the strangest, most distinctive poetic texts I've ever read: I abandoned the rudimentary desire for a coherent account.

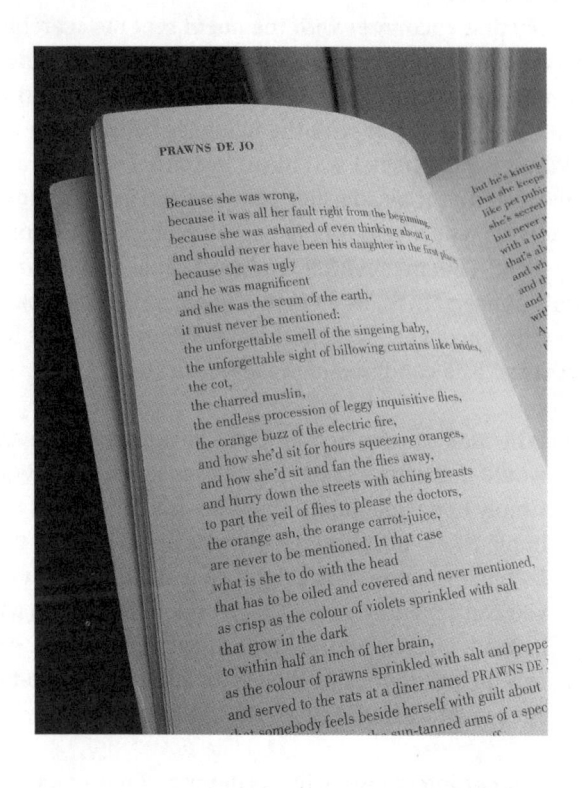

The poem that most excites me in *Bunny* is 'PRAWNS DE JO'. The other poems in the collection are for the most part short, and I enjoy them also, but 'PRAWNS DE JO' is the kind of poem I can read over and over, and would most like to be able to write myself. It's a craggy, uninhibited text ailing under the weight of its own images that enact — collectively — a pathology of trauma. It is the first mention of hair in the collection and, to my mind, the moment of the narrative of *Bunny* in which the first transgression is made by the lodger (the next poem, 'Mussels', shows 'a pair of soiled electric-blue pyjamas' soaking 'like mussels' in a sink).

My first encounter with the poem sent me searching for an interview with Hill I'd previously read online. Asked by the interviewer, poet and academic Lidia Vianu, to say something about her life, Hill begins with the following: 'I was born in 1945. When I was a baby I was burnt in a fire. I was rescued from my burning cot by a farmer who saw the flames. I spent six months (maybe a year, I'm not sure) in hospital. Of course, I nearly died.' Like many other readers, I came to see *Bunny*, and Hill's entire oeuvre, as an embodiment of the 'concealment tangled with unconcealment' that Denise Riley identifies in 'Lyric Shame' as a condition of the affective state:

> Why make such a bother about it, though, when anyone would naturally expect that the sense of shame would simply keep you quiet? That line of thought says it's implausible and perverse to make a noise out of the feeling of shame. However, if your shame is such that you can't manage to speak, you might be able to *write*, instead. Literary writing may function, for some, exactly as a means of *not* speaking — of avoiding face-to-face speech altogether.

Indeed, in other interviews, Hill has described her poems as veiled references to her own life and trauma — 'if I wanted to say something unkind about somebody I would turn them into an animal and then even possibly change their gender in order to encode them in some way so it wasn't so direct' — and, in another poem in a previous collection (*Aeroplanes of the World*), writes, 'The first man I attracted / was my father, / who people said was young / ... But actually he wasn't. He was old. / I told my little friends he was the lodger.'

When it comes to *Good Morning, Midnight*, Sasha's itinerancy, her drinking and general precarity seem to mirror what is known of the author's life. Her family history is, like that of *Bunny*'s speaker, murky — obliquely so. At the outset of the book, Sasha relates a dream in which 'a little man, bearded, with a snub nose, dressed in a long white night-shirt' speaks 'earnestly' to her, telling her, 'I am your father.... Remember that I am your father.' Promptly, she notices that 'blood is streaming from a wound in his forehead... "Murder," he shouts, "murder, murder",' and, in the dream, Sasha starts shouting too. She wakes up to the sound of a man singing out in the street. After this, there is little to no mention of family. There is, however, a singular passage about a hopeless kitten, which Sasha describes as having belonged to a couple who lived in the flat above her, back in London:

> The kitten had an inferiority complex and persecution mania and nostalgie de la boue and all the rest. You could see it in her eyes, her terrible eyes, that knew her fate. She was very thin, scraggy and hunted, with those eyes that knew her fate. Well, all the male cats in the neighbourhood were on to her like one o'clock. She got a sore on her neck, and the sore on her neck got worse.

Sasha takes the kitten in but becomes disgusted by it. She shoos the kitten out of her apartment and it flies into the street, where it is immediately run over by a taxi. What I want to say, but refuse to explain, is that I believe the kitten to be both Sasha and Sasha's mother (and perhaps, by extension, Rhys herself).

'Nostalgie de la boue', by the way, translates as 'nostalgia for mud'. Family might not always be the source of our shame, but family dictates how we deal with it. What is deemed shameful by ourselves is often what our parents, our grandparents deemed shameful. Patterns of shame can of course be broken, halted, but mostly they are carried on through, like mottos, or emotional heraldry.

It's clear that for Hill and for Rhys, for myself, shame, in life and in writing, is linked to abjection. In 'PRAWNS DE JO', self and other meet and merge in an experience that is both agonising and exciting, a shuddering pleasure-pain that is manifest in the hairpiece the speaker is 'secretly proud of because she is horrified by', that's 'always about to come skew and slither off'. I associate this part about the wig in Hill's poem with the moment in *Good Morning, Midnight* at which Sasha says of a woman that her 'red hair is arranged so carefully over her tiny skull'. In both Hill and Rhys these remarkable little pats of hair threaten to fly off or be otherwise displaced. Only they are not hair, they are disembodied hands. They are trapdoors that threaten to fly up and expose little black squares, admitting elements from the chaotic id into a reality governed by an opposing order. At another point in Rhys's novel, an old lady — 'past shame, detached, grim' — 'takes off her hat and she is perfectly bald on top — a white, bald skull with a fringe of grey hair'. The old woman is not cowed, but defiant. 'Come along, mother,' hisses her daughter, mortified, as her eyes meet Sasha's in a mirror.

In shame, just as other becomes self, past becomes present. *Good Morning, Midnight* moves back and forth in time in nauseating ebbs, segueing into a chilling self-awareness when Sasha says, 'You are walking along a road peacefully. You trip. You fall into blackness. That's the past — or perhaps the future.' (Or perhaps a psychic trapdoor?) It's the disap-pearance of these boundaries — what Elena Ferrante's Lila refers to in the Neapolitan Novels as 'dissolving margins' — that is at the sore heart of abjection. From Kristeva's *Powers of Horror*: 'the time of abjection is double: a time of oblivion and thunder, of veiled infinity and the moment when revelation bursts forth... abjection brings together fascination and shame, the clean and the filthy, the sought-after and the banished...'.

In the physiology of shame, blushing is the visible manifestation of this temporal collapse, for at the moment of blushing the reality of the shameful memory is experienced just as vividly as that of the present trigger. In *Affect Imagery Consciousness*, Silvan S. Tomkins describes the 'psychological dominance of the face' as a point of focus, given the 'relative density of neural representation' that occurs there. The cruelty of blushing is that it draws attention to the face, and so too to the self, that the subject is simultaneously prompted to conceal at all costs. As a physical response, blushing is the body's response to flight-or-fight situations: blood vessels dilate, increasing blood flow in order to deliver more oxygen to the head and brain, where it is thought to be most needed, causing the cheeks to turn red with the concentration of protein. The accompanying desire to hide the face from view is where the phrase to 'lose face', meaning to lose the respect of others, originates. In Homer's *Odyssey*, ashamed at her own betrayal of Menelaus, Helen refers to herself repeatedly as 'the dog-faced one' — her face is not lost, but marred, transformed into a shameful symbol. Selima Hill has spoken of her writerly shame, of feeling dirty and exposed when the boundary of the page collapses, revealing faces on both sides:

> I write for myself. I write for strangers. But when I meet real people face to face I feel trapped — as if I am a bad person. Ugly. Dirty. Inadequate. (Not at all the person I feel I am when I am writing, the person who is one with all things!)

In *Good Morning, Midnight*, Sasha cannot forget her face. Every time she ducks into a toilet to escape from the crowds outside she is met with a 'glass', and the discrepancy that she sees reflected there, between prior and current selves is, for her, a repetitive source of shame. 'Well, well,' the mirror says to her on such occasions, 'last time you looked in here you were a bit different, weren't you? Would you believe me that, of all the faces I see, I remember each one, that I keep a ghost to throw back at each one — lightly, like an echo — when it looks into me again?'

Looking back through *Bunny* to corroborate my story about the form of 'PRAWNS DE JO' I can see that there are a few other poems of a similar shape in the collection. 'PRAWNS DE JO', however, maintains its particular appeal. It's the eye of the book, in my opinion. It's a scar, but not one that has healed well — it's sensitive and it's purple, and if you touch it too hard with a nail it will open. In fact, the poem might yet be an open wound, a sticky orange wound covered over with a stubborn orange glob of coagulated body resin that looks disgusting and smells too. Miniscule hairs have gathered inside it and migrated to the wound's edges, giving it a black outline. Perhaps it will never heal. Perhaps Hill does not want it to: there's awful pleasure to be taken in manipulating one's wounds.

      Today I pulled some fine, white hairs from a weeping wound on the back of my heel. Mammals in general are prone to over-troubling their wounds. One theory is that excessive licking causes endorphin release, which reduces pain and makes the animal feel temporarily euphoric. But too much touching or licking of wounds can produce painful lesions that distort the skin and invite infection. You may have an infection if the wound area becomes dark and dry, or bigger and deeper. At school, in the boring classes, I would sometimes preoccupy myself by creating highly realistic wounds on my hands using red, brown, green, yellow and grey markers.

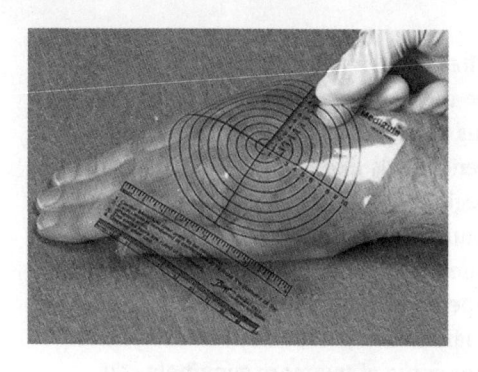

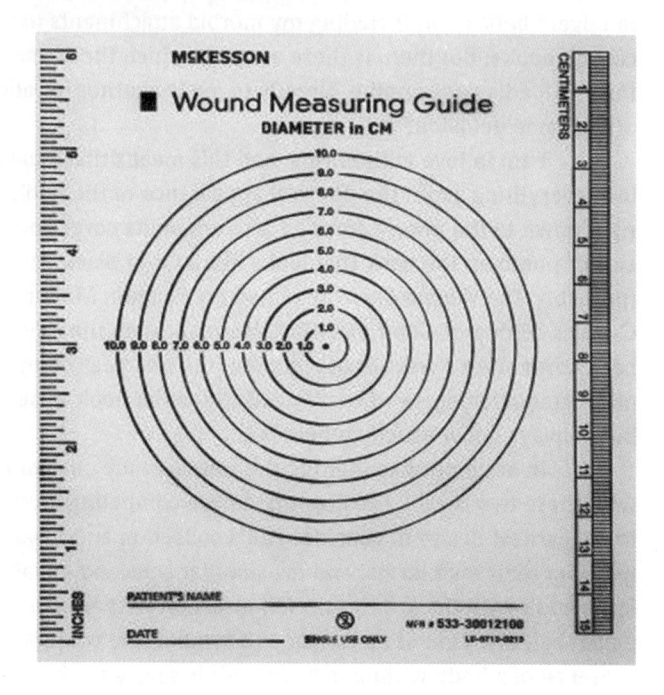

Can we anticipate trauma? Sometimes I wonder. I had my first panic attack aged thirteen, when it suddenly seemed to me that someone had fixed tight elastic bands around both of my wrists. Then I couldn't breathe. No discernible cause.

A close friend of mine has written a poem after 'PRAWNS DE JO', and I think we love the poem for a lot of the same reasons, but the fact of both of us publicly acknowledging the poem as a direct source of influence feels like fighting. As with each of my favourite books I begin to develop possessive feelings about *Bunny* as an object (it must stay close by) and to believe that there is something in the text that is speaking to me personally. One day, during a Wikipedia jaunt, I read about magical thinking and its relationship to narcissistic personality disorders, and worry that this describes some of my more genuinely self-indulgent behaviour, including my morbid attachments to certain books. But then, is there a way in which the sense that the Wikipedia page applies directly to me is another iteration of the same delusion?

I am in love with *Bunny*, and this means that I soon love everything about the physical appearance of the book, right down to the poorly cropped artwork on its cover and Hill's author photo on the back that looks like a Goya Black Painting (probably *The Witchy Brew*). I've had my Penguin Modern Classics edition of *Good Morning, Midnight* with the metallic back cover since I was about eighteen (the first year of my undergraduate degree). I don't need to see the book as such, but I always know exactly where it is.

In attempting to identify the source of my obsession with these two books, I realise that I have competing interests in my earnest desire to consider Hill's collection and Rhys's novel on their own terms, and my simultaneous and equally felt fascination with these authors' self-insertion in their work, for which hair is a kind of metonym — a symbol that conjures the presence of a body without a body (hair is surely the body's diacritical mark). Veronica Forrest-Thomson writes that, even if written in the language of information, once text is presented as poetry, the 'I' is no longer a 'particular person'. 'For the purposes of the poem,' she states, 'the "I" is simply a voice.' The inverse supposition that equates poet with speaker has so often been wielded as a bludgeon against women's poetry. By linking the feats of women's work, often irrevocably, to the widely-accepted narratives of these poets' lives, critics smother the writing's 'technical innovation' by anxiously transforming 'all verbal organisation into extended meaning... pattern into theme' (surely a further manifestation of the equating of women's selves uniquely with women's bodies).

Good Morning, Midnight — like Penelope Mortimer's *The Pumpkin Eater*, like Jamaica Kincaid's *Lucy* or Lorrie Moore's *Anagrams* — is, to my mind, a kind of poem/novel hybrid, having practically nothing to do with the stifling instrumentalism of the well-plotted work of commercial fiction. In 'PRAWNS DE JO', the relentless anaphora and metaphorical questions ask us to read the text as a poem, a revelatory text, while the cataclysmic structure of the whole reveals it for what it is: a wedding — an actual wedding, of some kind, with its formal dress, expensive food, rituals, guilt, narcissism and self-doubt. But a wedding, also, of multiple points of traumatic origin, and so too of points in time, of figures, of sexualities, of linguistic registers. In both *Good Morning, Midnight* and *Bunny*, the 'I' ultimately 'remains enigmatical, presenting only the words on the page.' But I've barely approached the language of *Bunny* and *Good Morning, Midnight*, and it's to my shame that I myself have dirtied this demarcation between author and voice, especially with respect to Hill's work — but the defilement has also been deliberate. This is because I think that bringing these two impulses into direct contact with one another is in itself a form of abjection, that the friction generated here — between self and speaker, between blood and hair and page — might be what needs to be touched on, presently; this crawl space between id and ego, this wire fence pitted wilfully along the imaginary border between the instrumental and the whimsical.

For a while now I have been most interested in work that tries to access and/or articulate an abomination that has been named variously as 'emotional truth', 'literary truth' and simply 'the truth' by a number of modern and contemporary writers (though usually women). The expression refers not to the so-called 'factual' truth of any given situation (names, times, dates, events), but to an essential and transcendental truth. It is something I have seen best expressed by Elena Ferrante:

> It is not enough to say, as we are increasingly accustomed to do nowadays: these are events that truly happened, it's my real life, the names and last names are real, I'm describing the real places where the events occurred. Writing that is inadequate can falsify the most honest biographical truths. Literary truth isn't founded on any autobiographical or journalistic or legal agreement. It's not the truth of the biographer or the reporter or a police report or a sentence handed down by a court; it's not even the plausibility of a narrative constructed with professional skill. Literary truth is the truth released exclusively by words used well, and it is realised entirely in the words that formulate it. It is directly proportional to the energy that one is able to impress on the sentence. And when it works, there is no stereotype, cliché, worn baggage of popular literature that resists it.

Ferrante is by no means the first to identify this linguistic phenomenon, but what is unique in this passage is her venturing something to do with the actual *make-up* of the thing and its having something to do with syntax. My feeling is that perhaps there is a kind of parallel-running language that is similar to ours but that is not ours, and that when a writer manages — nearly, briefly — to access this paralanguage, we get a glimpse of what could be expressed if we were able to access this other, more frank (but likely bleak, likely barbaric) reality. My feeling is that Rhys and Hill and a limited number of other writers are able to access this paralanguage at will — a statement with which I only wish to highlight their skill with language, rather than undermine it. A final quote from Hill:

> The only energy we have is the energy of our own lives. But sometimes autobiography is not true enough. In order to be ruthlessly accurate (which is my aim) it is sometimes necessary to fictionalise: in this way I feel free.

WAYS (SELF-LOVE)

Instances of assault do affect women for some time after they happen,
but they often unleash an anger that has never been able to find
its target before, which is strengthening.

Learn to welcome intrusive thoughts. Invite them in,
entertain them for as long as you can stand to, quietly
tell them to leave.

Read a recent interview with Monica Lewinsky.
Read June Jordan's 'Poem about My Rights'.
Read and answer Audre Lorde's 'Questionnaire to Oneself'.
Read *Italian Women Poets*, edited by Biancamaria Frabotta.
Read Diane Wakoski's *Dancing on the Grave of a Son of a Bitch*.

Write a poem that is also a revenge fantasy.
Write a poem that is so full of hate.
Publish these poems in a collection and dedicate the book
to someone you love.

Understand the extreme creative potency of your thoughts.
The experience of shame itself indicates the presence,
whether realised or latent, of a powerful imagination.

Consider how the disaster links you in a deep and irrevocable way
to many other women.

Understand that in the time that has passed your attacker
has become an insect; he is terrified of you. He is consumed
by the things he has done, and he, unlike you, has cause to feel enduring,
burning, life-destroying shame.

Buy yourself something delicious to eat and eat it.
Allow yourself to really enjoy it.

WHOSE HAIR

I am sitting on the sofa stroking our new white kitten. I notice that she is licking her mouth in a way that suggests something is bothering her (it's not long since she's stopped teething). I inspect her mouth and immediately spot the culprit: not a loose tooth, but a short black hair caught up in the kitten's teeth and gums. I grasp the hair and pull, however as I do so it becomes immediately clear that the hair is not short, but very long, and it is coming from all the way down the kitten's throat. I pull and pull, and the hair keeps coming — the kitten gags. By the time I have retrieved the entire hair it measures about twenty centimetres long. It is thick, dark, doused in saliva. I stare at the hair, shocked. The kitten wanders off. After just three seconds or so a pressing question forms: whose hair *is* this?

It takes a friend to remind me of a simple fact: 'Didn't you used to have long black hair?' she writes in an email. 'It seems the cat was in the process of ingesting one of your former selves.'

8

LASTING ANGER

I work at my desk at the bay window in my flat on the first floor. Everyone who walks down this street — without exception — knows when they are being watched. One woman — neatly dressed but casual, mobile but seeming extremely ill — stopped dead in her tracks. She looked about the street. She couldn't locate the thread of my gaze. She was too ill to raise her head. Her face — eyes, lips, nose, hair — was all one colour.

Andrew, a black and mostly white cat, crosses and crosses the narrow road, back and forth all day. Sometimes he ends up down by the church. Both pavement and road are covered in dark, uneven patches that make them look as though they have been somehow wetted and are drying off. Every morning I look out of my bedroom window with the same view and think that it has been raining while I was asleep.

The funny thing about Andrew: he is out all the time and appears very bold on his street corner, however if you approach him he becomes nervous, meows — not in a hysterical way, but certainly a bit pathetic — and moves quickly away. You see his face close up and his eyes are pink and watery and have specks of dirt and mucus around them, but from far away he appears sleek, confident. Every time I move away I forget his wet eyes and his nervousness, and every time I approach him again I see it clearly and am freshly perturbed.

A few months ago, at a bus stop on the other side of town, I was cornered by a man. He was very drunk and he was, of course, abrasive, though only in the way of an inebriated male stranger who understands those around them (young women especially) as owing them the exact response they decide in that moment to want. His eyes were glowing and changing shape before me — it hurt to look at them directly. I spoke to him in the way I have cultivated for such scenarios. He needed something from our exchange. He supposed I was uninformed and, as I stepped onto my bus, told me to watch Al Jazeera.

The motion sickness comes and goes but it no longer frightens me in quite the same way. Against the odds, I have found myself able to read, to write — to think. And a new vision — as compulsive, as fervid as the monkeys — has begun to affirm itself in my consciousness...

    A woman is in a house, in a living room. The house has low ceilings. It's dim inside. The woman hears a noise. She gets up from where she has been sitting, keeping her index finger in the book she has been reading so as not to lose her place. She carries the book with her in one hand as she walks through to the kitchen. As soon as she enters the small kitchen she is met with the surprise of a bonfire in the back garden, which she can see through the wide window above the sink. She continues walking, stepping into the rectangular garden of indeterminate size. She pulls the book she is carrying towards herself, resting it on her chest, still with her finger in it. Still with her finger in it, she regards the other women in the garden. (There are other women in the garden.) The other women are all watching the bonfire. The bonfire is tall. It makes a racket. It whips up the air around it, tossing the women's hair about as though there were a fierce arctic wind passing through, but the air beyond the fire's atmosphere is really very still.

At first I think that the women surrounding the bonfire must be burning their books, are about to toss the paperbacks and cloth-bound volumes onto the bonfire, but this is not the case. They all rest the books on their chests, keeping their places with a finger, like the woman who has just left the house for the garden. They appear content to watch the fire and are all very still. What is fuelling the fire? Nothing: the fire fuels itself. The fire *is* the fuel. The fuel is anger, and the anger is personal and it is cultural — an inheritance. I understand this better when I encounter an interview with Italian poet Anna Malfaiera in which she refers to 'the so-called "lasting anger"':

> What has been a stimulus is the conviction that women must wage two wars: the one to establish their own identity and the one to assert themselves as producers of values in the present situation. Women's current self-analysis in all the countries of the world has an incalculable importance on every level. The so-called 'lasting anger' still exists, perpetuates itself, and grows for those same reasons that give rise to it.

In *Poetic Artifice*, Forrest-Thomson relates a particular instance of Ted Hughes undermining Sylvia Plath's work via his own limited perspective: 'He says of "Last Words" in her book *Crossing the Water*, "it is a poem which would have been safer said by a persona in some kind of play."' 'Perhaps so,' writes Forrest-Thomson, 'if we are concerned with Sylvia Plath the individual, although the comment shows an inappropriate idea of a poet's relation to his poems even as "lyrical utterance": it demonstrates the notion that the woman who suffers cannot relieve her suffering by becoming the mind which creates...'.

A woman who suffers can indeed relieve her suffering by becoming the mind which creates: creates worlds, creates texts, creates herself; creates personal/private/public space(s) and, via the latter, other women. This is a final affirmation, then: *a woman who suffers can relieve her suffering by becoming the mind which creates.* And that is exactly what I believe we must do.

AFTERWORD FOR THE SECOND EDITION

I wrote this book in 2016 and 2017, when I was coming out of a period of acute difficulty; I found myself in a position in which I had to write the book I needed in order to do so. It's therefore a bit strange, perhaps, to have been surprised – I was, I am – to have learned that it has helped other people, too; to hear this, now and again, is my greatest happiness.

Looking over it now, I recognise a strong desire in myself to re-enter the text and to smooth certain things over, to make certain phrases and passages clearer, to correct my grammar. But I don't have the energy. And there is something affirming, too, about acknowledging these lapses and errors while allowing them to remain in place.

My only true addendum is on the question of silence, which has become, for me, an increasingly complicated idea – both in and of itself and as it pertains to the notion of self-protection. I include hereafter two pieces written in 2018 and 2021, respectively, a poem and a short prose text. The style of the latter corresponds to that of *small white monkeys* (particularly the later sections of the book). These two pieces offer differing thoughts on the question of silence as a reactive token, both as a form of complicity and of intimacy.

– SC, August 2021

THANK YOU FOR YOUR HONESTY

A response to digital prints, animations and texts by Niamh Riordan

1)

To disturb reality using
its own means
and not a subjective interpretation thereof
presenting the viewer with an image
more abject – in the truer sense of the word –
than another kind
which displays contrivances to discomfit her
It is a pure expression of hope

a challenge to the natural order
the moral framework of material honesty
which prizes marble over stucco
a hierarchy with no equivalent
in poetry (though undoubtedly we will it), in which
a stated allegiance
to 'truth' and '"the functioning(s)" of "language"'
coupled with any broad effect of semantic cohesion
is usually enough (if
issued from the correct source)

Analogical infirmity
consciously acknowledged
confounds the 'flow'
Still I am forced to ask the disingenuous question,
Is marble alive?

Without a metabolism, cells
or the ability to achieve homeostasis, no

2)

To perform bemusement again and again
as a waiving of authority
(and so too of blame)

Honesty in a community of what is thought of as
blameless self-interest
makes you cry a lot, even (especially?) in instances
where it manifests in harm done to you and to others
via indirect means
for that too (the action) is honesty

(and perhaps a more fundamental kind)

3)

Flashes
in the centre of my field of vision
are gentle
cannot be said to increase or decrease in frequency
over time
Doctors don't worry much about such disturbances

Asked the same question of an adult in childhood
surmised from the response
a theory of germs within the retina
as magnified by the eye's lens

9

SILENCE

Think about silence and all it implies. But think – now, quickly – about words and meaning. About words and meaning and metaphor. About words and deception. About how metaphor – or any kind of figurative language – might, in fact (and often inadvertently), lead to a kind deception. Think about how speech – as opposed to silence – might effect an inadvertent (self-)deception.

    Think of a scaffold. I have a fondness for scaffolds. On mentioning, however, in any given situation, my liking for these structures, talk tends to turn first (though not always) to provisionality, to the scaffold's transitory nature. In her 'Notes Toward a History of Scaffolding', poet Susan Mitchell dubs scaffolds ephemeral, 'dross from the furnace'.

    But unlike dross, a mass of solid impurities floating on molten metal post smelting, the scaffold, in assisting with the resurrection and upkeep of buildings and artworks, does not undergo any permanent, substantive change itself. A scaffold is neither a catalyst nor a waste material; it maintains its own shape, even after its deliberate collapse.

A second line of conversation (though not always): the scaffold is likened to [x]. It becomes an analogy – for the importance of aid, often. <u>For the importance of institutional aid.</u> And a metaphor, too, for the artistic process, as opposed to its product. Sometimes, the former likeness is communicated in the tones of a thought-terminating statement – usually, a cliché invoked in order to quell any cognitive dissonance the speaker might be experiencing. *It is what it is.*

The mind reaches for clichés, for thought-terminating statements, when it perceives insurmountable difficulties and/or a problem whose resolution might leave the individual to whom it occurs in a position – ostensibly – of lower security (as with, say, wealth redistribution).

Mmm, yes, such vital work.

Sometimes, when a metaphor feels apt enough, satisfying both speaker and audience with its apparent accuracy, it can become a kind of decoy, supplanting the original need for a real, a more complex solution.

One day, while looking through an artist's book with a friend, I notice myself drift, as I always do – as I have taught myself to do – towards the more incongruous, idiosyncratic pieces. Towards those pieces that would, offered alone and without qualifications, misrepresent the larger, so-called body of work.

'That one,' I say, stabbing at a smallish image towards the bottom of a verso page. 'I like that one.'

The page I have selected is full of decorative borders: frames and scrolls that presage nothing. These empty labels imply text, suggesting, through their arrangement, the planned presence of a verbal sign without committing to anything so limiting, such that the reader is left to contemplate the silence, as when, in conversation, the listener remains mute, but, through her deferral of speech, offers her silence as a reactive token – that is, as an indication of displeasure, disagreement, embarrassment...

My friend remains silent. But her silence signals none of the above. I take it in, the silence. In this instance, my finger still on the page, my friend still mute, the silence strikes me as a condition of our intimacy, as a thorough and felt engagement with my statement and with our shared view of the book, the page. It is a rejection of cliché, of a desire to name or decide. To make a value judgement. To grip and pincer. To assent or contradict. Her silence tells me that I am no threat to her.

Silence is not the opposite of speech. <u>There is no such thing as silence.</u>

NOTES

small white monkeys was commissioned by Book Works in collaboration with Glasgow Women's Library as part of the former's You Must Locate A Fantasy library residency scheme, which enables artists and writers to work with libraries, special collections and archives throughout the UK.

Glasgow Women's Library is the only accredited museum in the UK dedicated to women's lives, achievements and histories. The library's archives include the Scottish Women's Aid archives, the Women's Suffrage Collection and the Scottish and National Abortion Campaign archives, as well as archives of artists' work, including the Dorothy Dick and Hannah Frank collections.

The essay(s) and poems in this book were made through research into Glasgow Women's Library's materials and resources, and with the help of the library's staff and the library's atmosphere of support. I started in the Violence Against Women archives, which include records from the Edinburgh and Glasgow Rape Crisis Centres, and the Zero Tolerance archives. I began my research by compiling a document of first-person accounts and testimonies pertaining to experiences of sexual violence and associated trauma. The result was something akin to Svetlana Alexievich's polyphonic historical writings and, although it remains unpublished, the voices gathered in this document helped me to find my own. Some of the poems in this book contain fragments or derive their structures from treated archive material, including public information sheets and pamphlets. Much of the writing of *small white monkeys* took place in the Glasgow Women's Library, both in the Lending Library, where I was helped by the extensive collection of books by, for and about women (particularly the self-help texts and Women's Press books), and on the mezzanine level, where archive materials can be accessed.

Additional live and/or collaborative research was conducted throughout the residency via the public event 'On Shame and Writing: Work in Progress' with poet and novelist Daisy Lafarge, in April 2017, and in a closed writing group with authors Megan Nolan, Alanna McArdle and Amy Key, in June 2017.

Affirmations are taken from June Jordan's 'Poem About my Rights', Penelope Mortimer's *The Pumpkin Eater* and Audre Lorde's 'The Transformation of Silence into Language and Action' respectively.

Erica L. Johnson's article 'Haunted: Affective Memory in Jean Rhys's *Good Morning, Midnight*' helped me articulate some of my thinking about Rhys's novel.

The friend cited in the opening paragraph of OUR MOOD IS FAR MORE COMPLEX; OR, MIRRORS is Rebecca Tamás. An email from Emily Berry is cited in WHOSE HAIR. In HAIR PIECE I refer to Rachael Allen and her truth-filled poem 'Prawns of Joe'.

OTHER WORKS CITED ARE (IN ORDER OF FIRST APPEARANCE)

Chelsey Minnis, *Poemland* (Wave Books, 2009)

Anna Mendelssohn, *Implacable Art* (Salt, 2000)

Carolee Schneemann, 'The Breath of Life', *Art in America* (available online)

'Pet hating OAP admits poisoning five of his neighbours' cats using tuna laced with antifreeze', *Metro* (available online)

'Woman kills neighbour's cats with antifreeze to stop them urinating on her strawberries', *Daily Mail* (available online)

Sara Ahmed, *The Cultural Politics of Emotion* (Routledge, 2007)

Gabriele Taylor, *Pride, Shame and Guilt* (Oxford University Press, 1985)

Sandra Lee Bartky, *Femininity and Domination* (Routledge, 1990)

Gershen Kaufman, *The Psychology of Shame* (Routledge, 1993)

Sara Ahmed, *The Promise of Happiness* (Duke University Press, 2010)

Sheila Ernst and Lucy Goodison, *In Our Own Hands* (Women's Press, 1981)

Simone Weil, *Gravity and Grace* (Routledge, 2002)

Adrian Piper, *Everything #4*, 2004. Oval mirror with gold leaf-engraved text in traditional mahogany frame. Edition of 8. 13" x 10" (33 x 25.4 cm). Collection Adrian Piper Research Archive Foundation Berlin. © Adrian Piper Research Archive Foundation Berlin. († Page 45)

Denise Riley, *Impersonal Passion* (Duke University Press, 2005)

Vahni Capildeo (transcription), 'Podcast', *Scottish Poetry Library*

Denise Riley, 'Lyric Shame', *Shame and Modern Writing* (Routledge, forthcoming 2018)

Nuar Alsadir, 'Unknowing', forthcoming in *Studies in Gender and Sexuality* (2018)

Jean Rhys, *Smile Please* (Penguin, 1979)

Ana Mendieta in an interview with Eva Cockcroft, *Art and Artists* (February 1983)

Lisa Robertson, interview with *Canadian Women in the Literary Arts* (available online)

Selima Hill in an interview with Lucy Winrow, *The Construction of Gender through Embarrassment, Shame and Guilt in the Poetry of Selima Hill* (Winrow's unpublished doctoral thesis, University of Salford, 2014)

Jean Rhys, *Good Morning, Midnight* (Penguin, 2000)

Selima Hill, *Bunny* (Bloodaxe, 2001)

Veronica Forrest-Thomson, *Poetic Artifice* (Shearsman, 2016)

Julia Kristeva, *Powers of Horror* (Columbia University Press, 1982)

Silvan S. Tomkins, *Affect Imagery Consciousness* (Springer, 1962)

Elena Ferrante interview with Sandro and Sandra Ferri, *Frantumaglia* (Europa, 2016)

Selima Hill in an interview with Lidia Vianu (available online)

Anna Malfaiera cited in *Italian Women Poets*, ed. by Biancamaria Frabotta (Guernica, 2002)

IMAGE CREDITS

Pages 2–5 Representations of white monkeys, found online.

Page 9 Carolee Schneemann, *Eye Body: 36 Transformative Actions*, 1963.

Page 11 Carolee Schneemann, *Infinity Kisses – The Movie*, 2008.

Page 12 (1) Carolee Schneemann, *Infinity Kisses II*, 1990-1998, (2) Carolee Schneemann, *Fuses*, 1967.

Page 14 Representations of sleeping cats, found online.

Page 15 'Cat thwarts sex attack on owner', Scottish Women's Aid Archive, *Sunday Mail*, 19 May 1994, Glasgow Women's Library Archive.

Pages 21–22 'Feelings Words', Glasgow Women's Library Archive

Page 33 Hill Street premises, Garnethill, 1991, Glasgow Women's Library Archive.

Page 35 (1) Preparation for 'Women and Food' performance, September 1990, (2) Computer Training, Trongate, 2001, Glasgow Women's Library Archive.

Page 36 (1) Lesbian Avengers protest outside the Mitchell Library, 1996, (2) Trongate, c.1999, Glasgow Women's Library Archive.

Page 37 (1) Women's Own Album Launch, September, 1990, (2) Untitled, Glasgow Women's Library Archive.

Page 38 (1) 'Setting Agendas for Change' Conference, September 1990, (2) Panto Most Horrid, 1992, Glasgow Women's Library Archive.

Page 39 (1) Garnethill, 1991, (2) Garnethill, c.1991-1994, Glasgow Women's Library Archive.

Page 40 Clearing of the Women In Profile premises, 1998, Glasgow Women's Library Archive.

Page 45 (1) Adrian Piper, *Catalysis IV*, 1970. Performance documentation: 5 silver gelatin prints, each 16 x 16 inches (40.6 x 40.6 cm). Detail: Photograph #3 of 5. Photo credit: Rosemary Mayer. Collection of the Generali Foundation, Vienna. © Adrian Piper Research Archive Foundation Berlin and Generali Foundation. (2) Adrian Piper, *Catalysis IV*, 1970. Performance documentation: 5 silver gelatin prints, each 16 x 16 inches (40.6 x 40.6 cm). Detail: Photograph #5 of 5. Photo credit: Rosemary Mayer. Collection of the Generali Foundation, Vienna. © Adrian Piper Research Archive Foundation Berlin and Generali Foundation.

Page 55 'Judith and Her Maidservant', Artemisia Gentileschi, c. 1613-1614, Palazzo Pitti, Florence.

Page 61 'PRAWNS DE JO', in Selima Hill's *Bunny* (Bloodaxe, 2001). Photograph Sophie Collins.

Page 67 Wound measuring guide, found online.

NOTES TO THE PREFACE

1 Jacqueline Rose, 'To Die One's Own Death', *London Review of Books,* Vol. 42 No. 22 (November 2020) <https://www.lrb.co.uk/the-paper/v42/n22/jacqueline-rose/to-die-one-s-own-death>.
2 Helen Charman, 'Where does the shame go? On Sophie Collins' *small white monkeys*', *The Cambridge Humanities Review* 13 (Lent 2018).
3 Lauren Berlant, 'Trauma and Ineloquence', *Cultural Values*, Vol. 5 No. 1, 41-58, p.43.
4 Denise Riley, 'Lyric Shame', in *Shame and Modern* Writing, ed. Barry Sheils and Julie Walsh (London: Routledge, 2018), pp. 68-72, p. 69.
5 Riley, 'Dark Looks', *Selected Poems* (London: Reality Street, 2000), p.74.
6 See Sara Ahmed, 'Killing Joy: Feminism and the History of Happiness', *Signs*, Vol. 35, No. 3 (Spring 2010), 571-594.
7 Sara Ahmed, 'Knocking at the Door: Complaints and Other Stories about Institutions', Online Lecture, Glasgow School of Art, Tuesday, 16 February 2021. See also Sara Ahmed, *Complaint!* (Durham, NC: Duke University Press, 2021).

THANKS

Enormous thanks are due to Glasgow Women's Library, and to all of its staff and volunteers, especially Adele Patrick, Katie Reid, Nicola Maksymuik, Laura Dolan and Wendy Kirk.

Thank you to my editors, Jane Rolo and Huw Lemmey, and to Gavin Everall, at Book Works. Thank you Erik Hartin for the book design. And thanks to my friend and agent, Harriet Moore.

Thanks to all those who contributed to the launch of the first edition at South London Gallery, March 2018, and to Lizzie Homersham, Book Works, for her work on the second edition.

Thank you to Daisy, for important conversations and for introducing me to Adrian Piper's work; to Harry, for leading me to the Carolee Schneemann piece; to Sarah, for talks on affectless women and their writing; to Rebecca M. J., for telling me about Helen; to Lucy, for allowing me to read and cite from your original research on Selima Hill.

This book is also dedicated to Nora, Sara, Rachael, Jess, Livia, Alanna, Amy and Megan.